Charles County Public Library
www.ccplonline.org

THE CRIMS #3:
THE CRIMS AT SEA

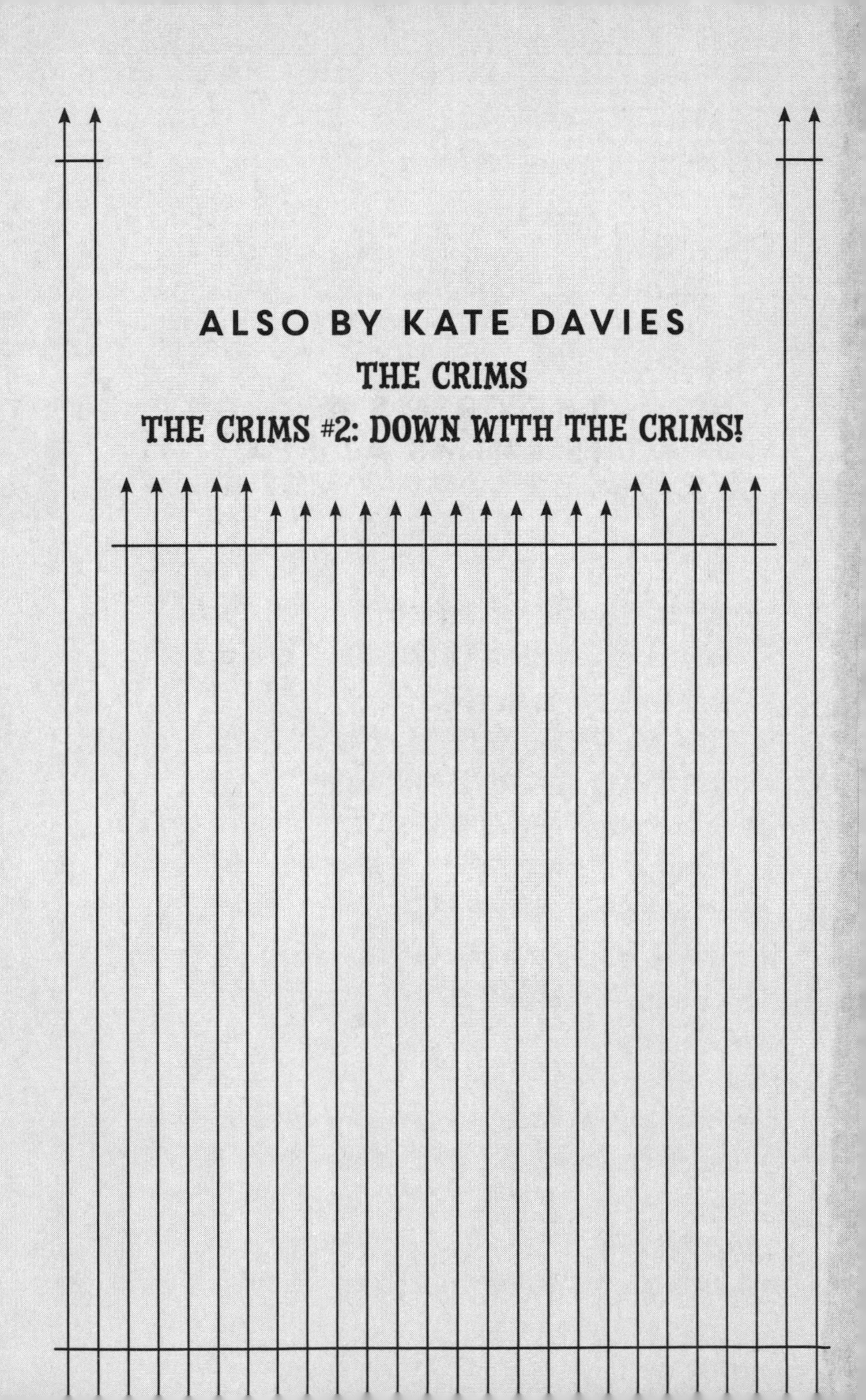

ALSO BY KATE DAVIES

THE CRIMS

THE CRIMS #2: DOWN WITH THE CRIMS!

THE CRIMS #3

THE CRIMS AT SEA

KATE DAVIES

HARPER
An Imprint of HarperCollins*Publishers*

The Crims #3: The Crims at Sea

Copyright © 2019 by Working Partners Ltd.
All rights reserved. Printed in the United States of America. No part of this book may be used or reproduced in any manner whatsoever without written permission except in the case of brief quotations embodied in critical articles and reviews. For information address HarperCollins Children's Books, a division of HarperCollins Publishers, 195 Broadway, New York, NY 10007.
www.harpercollinschildrens.com

Library of Congress Control Number: 2019947147
ISBN 978-0-06-249416-0

Typography by Sarah Nichole Kaufman
19 20 21 22 23 PC/LSCH 10 9 8 7 6 5 4 3 2 1
❖
First Edition

For Anna and William, for when they're older

THE CRIMS #3: THE CRIMS AT SEA

IMOGEN CRIM STARED at her phone, rereading the text message she'd just received: **Hey, loser, stealing a Norwegian Cruise liner. Party time in the Caribbean! You in?**

Even though the text was from an unknown number, she knew exactly who had sent it: Ava Kruk, her former nemesis and current best friend. Ava was the only person in the world capable of stealing a cruise ship single-handed, apart from maybe Big Nana, but Big Nana always said, "Never steal a vehicle designed for tourists. There's always a risk there will be a Celine Dion impersonator onboard."

Imogen would have loved to join Ava on a Norwegian cruise to the Caribbean—she loved nothing more than eating herring while listening to old Bob Marley records—but she was busy. So she texted back: **Sounds fun, but I can't. Kind of in the middle of something . . .**

A heist, to be exact. A heist that she had planned herself, with the help of her irritating but criminally talented cousin Delia. A proper heist, designed to get the Crims' street cred back. The Crims were supposed to be a terrifying crime family. But they'd had so much positive media attention since they chased the Kruks—a much more terrifying crime family—out of Blandington that they had lost all their cred. Even their schoolyard cred and their convenience store cred. People had started to stop the Crims in the street to shake their hands, which definitely made a change from having rotten tomatoes hurled at them, and the *Blandington Times* had run the headline: "Crims Save Blandington from International Crime Ring!"

Imogen's mother, Josephine, had been thrilled by this—she loved publicity and the word "ring," though she preferred her rings to be of the stolen diamond variety—but Imogen was frustrated. She hadn't actually meant to save Blandington from the Kruks. In fact, the Kruks had never really been a threat to Blandington at all. They were far too busy stealing major London landmarks to use as interior decor to bother committing crimes in such an insignificant town. Imogen had just been trying to save her family. Elsa Kruk, a children's book–obsessed psychopath who seemed unpleasantly fond of feeding people to tigers, had kidnapped them all, but a headline like "Girl Saves Her Own Family and Doesn't Really Care About Anyone Else in Blandington" probably wouldn't have sold as many papers.

Now the Crims were practically national treasures, like Kate Middleton and the crown jewels and fish and chips. And no one's scared of fish and chips. (Apart from Uncle Knuckles, who once had a very traumatic experience in a potato patch involving a sharp trowel and a lot of mud.) If a crime family isn't scary, it's basically just a family—an ordinary, boring family like every other family in Blandington—and, as Big Nana always said, "There's nothing worse than being ordinary and boring. Except being dead. Because then you'll be boring anyway; corpses never have much to say for themselves."

So, Imogen had taken things into her own hands. Things like walkie-talkies and loot bags and several extremely flattering balaclavas. She and Delia had masterminded a proper heist. A heist that would restore the Crims' reputation as hardened, if slightly eccentric, criminals. Imogen was getting on unusually well with Delia at the moment. Apart from Big Nana, Delia was the one other member of the family with any true criminal potential, as far as Imogen was concerned. At fourteen years old, Delia was still not *quite* as good as Imogen, who was only twelve, but hey, some people were late bloomers. The night they'd stayed up putting the final details to the plan had reminded Imogen of the bad old days, when the Kruks had been plotting to kill them all, and everyone had thought Big Nana was dead. Now stage one of the heist was underway.

Imogen looked at Delia and grinned. "You ready?" she said.

"Of course," said Delia.

And they walked over to their other cousins, the Horrible Children, who were standing outside the back entrance to Mega Deals, Blandington's biggest and least exciting electronics store, waiting for their orders.

"Does everyone know what they're supposed to be doing?" asked Imogen.

"Yes," said seven-year-old Nick. "I'm going to collapse on the ground and pretend to faint, to distract the store clerks."

"And then I'm going to collapse on the ground too, and the store clerks will think they're seeing double and get really confused," said Nate, Nick's identical twin.

"And I'm going to prank call the store and pretend to be Barry White," said Sam. He was thirteen, and his voice had just broken, which meant he was now much easier to understand but much less easy to make fun of.

Delia twirled a lock of curly hair around her finger and rolled her eyes. "No one under the age of forty knows who Barry White is."

"Luckily, the youngest store clerk is forty-five," said Sam. "And she has a tattoo of Barry White on her upper arm."

"How do you even know that?" asked Delia.

"People put way too much information about themselves on social media these days," said Sam, shrugging.

"I bite ankles!" Isabella babbled happily.

"Not everyone's ankles," Imogen said firmly. "Just the store clerks'." She'd had enough of her youngest cousin gnawing at her body parts. Isabella, at three years old, had precociously sharp teeth.

Freddie, Imogen's eldest cousin, nodded. "And when the clerks' backs are turned, me, Imogen, and Delia will steal all the electronics in the store."

"Except the Why?Phones," said Imogen. "Don't bother with them." (The Why?Phone was Mega Deals's own brand of smartphone, and it was so terrible that no one knew why it existed, hence its name.) Imogen looked at the checklist she was holding. "Freddie, did you remember to rent a getaway van?"

Freddie rolled his eyes. "Of course I did," he said. "Remember: I remember everything. How Big Nana takes her tea [nine sugars], Uncle Clyde's birthday [Christmas Eve], the date that Julius Caesar was assassinated—March 15, 45 BC—"

"No! It was 44 BC!" said Isabella, who watched a lot of documentaries. She launched herself at Freddie's ankles, and he let out a yelp.

"And then, as everyone is running out of the store, I'll set fire to it," said twelve-year-old Henry, flicking his lighter in preparation.

Imogen smiled. "Perfect. Everyone playing to their strengths."

"Can we get on with the heist now?" asked Delia, who was always bored when she wasn't the center of attention.

"Just a second," said Imogen. "Let me disable the security system. . . ."

She crowbarred open the back door to Mega Deals and found a box, helpfully marked "Security System." She pulled down a lever, conveniently marked "Disable." Imogen was almost disappointed. *They could have made it a bit more of a challenge.*

"Okay," she whispered. "Me, Freddie, and Delia will sneak in the back way. The rest of you, go to the front entrance. Send Isabella in first . . . People think she's cute, for some reason, so they won't pay attention to the rest of you. . . ."

As the Horrible Children set off for the front entrance,

Imogen felt the rush she always felt when she was committing a felony with members of her family. She hadn't felt this rush for far too long. She grinned at Delia. "I don't like to sound sentimental," she said, "but it turns out working with you doesn't suck."

Delia grinned back. "Working with you doesn't suck, either. Except when we're planning heists involving Popsicles, obviously."

"Obviously," said Imogen. She beckoned Freddie over and tossed him and Delia the balaclavas that Aunt Bets had knitted for them. "Right," she said. "Let's steal some HDTVs we don't need."

The heist started smoothly enough. Nick and Nate were walking past the home audio section when they collapsed, very convincingly, on the floor at exactly the same time. The clerks rushed to help them, leaving the electronic goods—and the tills—unguarded.

"Whoa," said a booming store clerk, looking from Nick to Nate and back again. "Are there two of them? Or did I eat too much cheese at the fondue party last night?"

"Both," said a large, frizzy-haired clerk. "There are definitely two of them. But you ate all the brie, and you left me with that boring lump of cheddar. Not cool."

While the store clerks were looking the other way, Imogen started to fill her loot bag with surprisingly expensive headphones. Out of the corner of her eye, she saw Delia and Freddie loading their bags with laptops.

"Well," boomed the clerk who had telling grease stains on her polo shirt, bending over Nick, who was imitating a carpet. "It's lucky we did that first aid course last week. . . ."

Imogen and Delia looked at each other. They hadn't counted on the clerks knowing how to do first aid.

"I've been dying to practice resuscitation!" said the frizzy-haired salesclerk, kneeling down next to Nate.

"And I'll do chest compressions on the other one!" said the booming salesclerk, cracking her fingers. "I might break a few of his ribs, but they'll sort that out when they get him to the hospital. . . ."

Which is when Nick and Nate staged miraculous recoveries at exactly the same time. It wasn't ideal, but Imogen didn't blame them.

Nick sat up and rubbed his eyes. "Where am I?" he said.

Nate stood up. "We suffer from narcolepsy," he said. "Don't we, Nick?"

Nick nodded. "A terrible affliction."

The clerks looked disappointed. "What a shame," said the frizzy-haired salesclerk. "I didn't get to do CPR! Or use an AED! Or any other acronyms!"

Imogen tried to catch Nick's attention. *Keep distracting*

them, she tried to say with her eyes. *Pretend to break your leg RIGHT NOW, or I'll come over there and do it for you.* But that's quite a hard thing to say with your eyes, so Nick just looked at her blankly.

And then it was too late. The salesclerks turned away from Nick and Nate—and came face-to-face with Imogen and Delia, who had their arms full of video game consoles and power drills.

Imogen and Delia froze like criminal snowmen.

The store clerks froze like law-abiding icicles.

They stared at one another for quite a long time. It was all a little bit awkward.

"Why hasn't Sam called the store?" Imogen whispered to Delia. "Is he even *more* incompetent now that his voice has broken? And why isn't Isabella biting anyone? Really, she's chosen this moment to stop being a miniature psychopath?"

"Don't worry, Henry's on the case," Delia said, nodding over to Henry, who was standing behind a salesclerk, desperately flicking his lighter and trying to start a fire. But the flame wasn't coming on. He'd obviously used up all the gas.

"He's literally as much use as a light bulb made out of socks," whispered Imogen. She was starting to panic. *What would Big Nana do?* she asked herself. Her grandmother would probably just try to ride this out—smile politely and walk out of the store, loot in hand—which almost certainly wouldn't work, but it wasn't as though Imogen had many other options. At the moment, she and Delia and the store clerks were still just standing there.

So Imogen smiled politely (not that the store clerks could tell, because she was, after all, wearing a balaclava) and walked, head held high, out of the store. And amazingly, the store clerks just stood there and watched her leave and then carried on with their jobs—pricing video games, ringing up purchases on the tills, pretending to know things about hard drives—as if nothing had happened. It was like she and Delia were invisible. Which they definitely weren't, because she could see Delia admiring her balaclava in the TV screens as they passed.

"That was weirdly easy," said Freddie, once they were out on the street.

"Weirdly is right," said Imogen. She looked around for the getaway van. There were two trucks in the street. One had a logo on the side: "EZTV." The other one had to be theirs— It had "Crims" written all over it. Literally. Spray-painted in Henry's handwriting.

"Henry," Imogen said as the other Crims came running out of the store after her, "it's not a great idea to write our name on the getaway van. We've been over this. The aim is not to get caught. Remember?"

"But you said you wanted us to get our street cred

back," Henry pointed out. "You can't get cred unless you take credit for your crimes."

"We want people to *think* we're dangerous but not be able to *prove* it," Imogen said as the Crims all scrambled into the van. She took the seat next to Freddie, who started the ignition, and turned to Sam, who was sitting behind her, wedged between the twins. "What happened to *you*? You were supposed to call the store and distract them for us!"

"Sorry," Sam said miserably. "I got a wrong number. First I accidentally dialed my math teacher, which was a shame, because it reminded him I hadn't finished my homework, and then I ended up singing 'You're the First, the Last, My Everything' to a pet shop owner in Nottingham for ten minutes."

Imogen heard footsteps behind the van. She looked into the rearview mirror—and there, running out onto the sidewalk, were the salesclerks. "Quick, Freddie, let's go!" she shouted. "They're shaking their fists at us. Excellent!" But then she looked at them again and realized that they were actually . . . waving.

As Freddie screeched away from the curb, Imogen felt a prickle of anxiety, and not just because she was sitting on Doom, Sam's nervous pet hedgehog. "Don't you think that was all a bit too easy?" she asked Delia, picking up the slightly squashed hedgehog and handing him back to Sam.

Delia pouted. "You're such a spoilsport. It *wasn't* too easy. We're just good at this!"

Imogen looked at Delia. How could she think that the heist had been a success? Everything that could have possibly gone wrong had gone wrong. Something, Imogen thought, was *up*. Any decent criminal would be feeling uneasy right about now. And if Delia wasn't, that meant she wasn't a decent criminal yet. Imogen sighed. She was sick of being dragged down by mediocre people. Even if those mediocre people did let her borrow their hair straighteners.

The van skidded to a halt outside Crim House, the Crims' exciting-looking but dangerous family home, which featured an extension made out of a bouncy castle, a garden mostly made up of plants stolen from cracks in the pavement (otherwise known as "weeds"), a lot of secret passageways that didn't lead anywhere, and a resident chicken that had escaped from an industrial poultry farm and wished it hadn't. Imogen's mother, Josephine, was on the doorstep, waiting for them. Which was, to say the least, unusual. Josephine was usually too busy "shopping" (i.e., stealing rich old women's jewelry) to notice when Imogen and her cousins came home. Or, indeed, when they'd been kidnapped.

"Darlings!" said Josephine, spreading her arms wide,

which looked like an effort; they were weighed down by diamond watches (two on each wrist); sapphire bracelets; and a live, rabid fox that she was wearing as a stole. Which was odd. Josephine liked luxury clothes, sure, but she usually saved the rabid fox for special occasions—the local dogs tended to attack her when she was wearing it. Odder still, Josephine wasn't alone. She had been followed out of the house by a group of people wearing headphones and carrying weird, unwieldy-looking pieces of equipment: a microphone, a camera, lights, a director's chair. . . . *Wait,* thought Imogen. *Why is there a camera crew at Crim House?*

Imogen stepped out of the getaway van and walked up the front path, her sternest look on her face. "Mum," she said. "What's going on?"

Josephine laughed a tinkling laugh, stroking the rabid fox's head. The fox foamed at the mouth and tried to bite her. "Surprise, my dears!" said Josephine. "Now that we've saved Blandington from the Kruks and become celebrities, I've signed us up to star in our very own reality TV series! Isn't that wonderful?"

"No," said Imogen.

Josephine ignored her. "Just think, darlings!" she said. "We'll be able to tell the world who we really are in our own words. Words like 'loving family' and 'criminal masterminds'—"

"And 'terrible parents,'" said Imogen, grabbing her

mother's sleeve and dragging her away from the cameras. "This is literally the worst idea you've ever had," she hissed. "And you once tried to steal the Duchess of Cornwall."

"No, darling, I tried to steal her *dress*. Her Royal Highness just happened to be wearing it at the time."

Imogen felt a prickling sensation on the back of her neck. She had the feeling she was being watched. She turned around and realized that the camera crew was filming her. "You can't use this footage," she said, putting her arm up to cover her face. "There's no way I'll sign the contract to appear in this stupid show."

"Silly Imogen!" tinkled Josephine. "You've already signed it!" She pulled the contract out from underneath her dangerous fur stole.

Imogen took the paper and studied it. There, in a variety of garish inks, were all the Crims' signatures. All forgeries, of course. Forgery was one of Josephine's specialties, crime-wise. "Now, excuse me, darling," she said. "You keep the camera crew company while I run upstairs and change into something a little more comfortable. Why don't you give them a tour of the grounds? They haven't met the snakes yet!" She touched the sound guy on the arm and said, "The boa constrictor's called Kevin, and he gives the loveliest hugs."

Josephine tottered inside on her stolen stilettos, leaving Imogen with the crew. Imogen took a closer look at the cameras. They had a logo on the side: "EZTV." The same logo she'd seen on the second van outside Mega Deals. . . .

Aha.

Things were starting to make sense. Maybe the crew had been involved in the Mega Deals heist? Perhaps the whole thing had been a setup. . . . In fact, that was probably the only reason they weren't all in jail right now.

"Look," she said to an overexcited woman with a clipboard. "None of us are going to talk to you. Are we?" she said, looking around for the rest of the Horrible Children. But her cousins were already giving interviews to different members of the TV crew. "Okay," said Imogen. "Maybe we *are* going to talk to you. But we won't say anything interesting."

The overexcited woman smiled at Imogen and shook her hand too hard. "I'm Belinda Smell," she said.

"Wow," said Imogen. "That's an . . . unusual name."

"I know," said Belinda Smell. "My ancestors ate a lot of French cheese."

Imogen guessed Belinda was a producer, because she kept producing things from her pockets. Things like chocolate bars and nondisclosure agreements and Imogen's childhood diary.

Imogen gasped and tried to snatch the diary back, but Belinda pulled it out of her reach. "Where did you get that?" Imogen asked.

"Your mum gave it to us," said Belinda. "We need as much background information about you as possible, to make sure the documentary feels really gritty and real! Gum?" She pulled a packet from her pocket.

"No, thank you," said Imogen, who always followed Big Nana's advice: "Never chew gum in front of strangers. Conserve your jaw strength in case you need to bite them."

But then Imogen's mother appeared at the front door again, wearing a silk nightdress and a new pair of (also stolen) stilettos and muttering, "This is my best side" and "Remember, soft lighting." She looked about as gritty as Isabella's mushed-up baby food, i.e., not gritty at all (except when Aunt Bets made it and added some broken glass to the mix to "toughen Isabella up"). Josephine was dragging her husband, Al, by the wrist, apparently trying to engage him in her *Real Housewives of Blandington* fantasy.

"Al!" she screamed at her husband. "How could you cheat like that?"

Al pushed his spectacles up his nose. "Cheat?" he said. "You mean on the mortgage application? It's really very simple. I just exaggerated my income—"

"Don't play innocent!" shrieked Josephine. "I *know* you're seeing Bets!"

She pointed at Aunt Bets, who had just appeared on the doorstep, holding some steel wool. She was knitting

Uncle Knuckles a suit of chain mail so that she could practice throwing axes at him.

Al blinked. "Of course I'm seeing her," he said simply. "She's standing right here."

Josephine let out a cry of frustration, and as usual, Al did all he could to comfort her, apologizing for not having affairs and promising to lie to her more often in the future.

The crew, probably sensing the drama was over, turned to Imogen. "Can we go inside?" Belinda asked her. "We'd love to get a one-on-one interview with you about the Mega Deals heist."

"I don't really want to take credit for my crimes on camera," said Imogen. "I'll get arrested, and I'm far too busy to go to jail. I have a crime empire to take over, and I still haven't seen the last season of *Gilmore Girls*."

"Don't worry!" said Belinda. "We can just use your first name, so no one will figure out who you are."

"Except that one of the policemen at the local station is my cousin, so he might guess," said Imogen.

But Belinda was pushing her through the hallway into the living room, and the camerawoman was pulling out an armchair for Imogen to sit in, and the sound guy was attaching a microphone to her shirt, and the lighting guy was shining a bright light into her eyes and telling her that green was her color.

"But I'm not wearing green," Imogen said, confused.

"I know," said the lighting guy, head to one side. "Shame."

"So!" said Belinda. "How about you choose a persona. Like are you the bad girl of the family? Or the ingénue? Are you the funny one? Or the one who always finishes the milk so that no one has anything to put on their breakfast cereal in the mornings?"

"Can't I just be myself?" asked Imogen.

Belinda made a face. "Boring," she said. "But don't worry! If you don't want to pick a personality, we'll choose one for you and put it together in the edit. Right. First let's get started. This was meant to be your big comeback heist. And the twins messed it up for you. How did you feel about that?"

Imogen had watched enough episodes of *Dancing with the Cars* (an extremely dangerous show in which competitors had to perform dance routines in the middle of highways) to know what was going on: The crew was trying to create conflict between the Crims, because families who get along make for extremely boring television. But Imogen wasn't going to play along. She smiled her best head girl of Lilyworth Ladies' College smile, which was a little rusty because she hadn't been head girl of Lilyworth Ladies' College for more than a year, and said, "The twins didn't mess it up. We got away from the store with more than a hundred thousand pounds' worth of electronics."

"Oh, come on," said Belinda. "You should hear what the twins told us about you. . . ." She looked around and said in a stage whisper: "Do you still sleep with a photograph of the Hatton Garden robbers under your pillow?"

"No, actually," said Imogen. "It's a poster, and it's on the wall above my bed." She made a mental note to punish the twins once the interview was over—trick them into getting paper cuts, or something. They clearly didn't know what loyalty meant. Which was understandable, considering Henry had set fire to the *L–Z* section of the dictionary.

"Let's change the subject," Imogen said, smiling. "Want me to tell you about how I get in shape before a big heist? It involves a straitjacket and a lot of dormice."

"I want you to tell me everything you hate about your family. Go on! Be mean! It suits you."

Imogen frowned. Why was Belinda trying to cast her as the villain when she was so obviously the heroine? "I'm not going to bad-mouth my family," said Imogen, her nose in the air.

"Okay, then," said Belinda, leaning forward. "How about bad-mouthing someone *else's* family? Why don't you tell me how you feel about what happened to the Kruks?"

Imogen's frown deepened. "What do you mean what happened to them?" she asked. "I feel fine about them leaving Blandington, obviously. One of them tried to feed my family to the sharks, and everyone knows you shouldn't overfeed sharks—it gives them diabetes. Plus, they stole all the bananas from Blandington Grocery, which meant the ice cream shop had to start serving potato splits."

"Actually," said Belinda, but she didn't say anything else, because that's when the front door banged open and Big Nana appeared by the living room door, hands on her extremely wide and dangerous-looking hips, saying, "What's going on here, then, you genetically modified passion fruits?"

"Ask Mum," Imogen said as Josephine bustled into the living room expensively.

"We're just filming a little television show," said Josephine, trying to sound casual.

"No you're not," said Big Nana, and she picked up the sound guy's boom and broke it over her knee.

"Don't worry," the sound guy said. "I have a spare."

"But do you have spare INTERNAL ORGANS?" asked Big Nana. "Because you'll need them when I've hanged, drawn, and quartered you! Don't think I don't know how! It's amazing what you can learn from the History channel. Now get out of my house!"

The sound guy ran for the door . . . but Belinda Smell held out her hand to stop him.

"We would love to leave," she said, producing the signed contracts from her pocket. "But these contracts are extremely, legally binding. As binding, in fact, as titanium ropes."

"The strongest kind of ropes," muttered Big Nana. She held out her hand for the contracts.

"Indeed," said Belinda. "If you just look at clause three, paragraph two . . ."

Big Nana's brow furrowed as she studied the small print. "'If the Interviewees try to eject the Crew from their house by threatening them with disembowelment, hanging, or any other form of execution, the Production Company hereby reserves the right to force all Interviewees to dress up in pink rompers and perform a fully choreographed dance routine to "We Are Family" on *The Public Humiliation Show*,'" she read. She looked up at Belinda, eyes narrowed. "But that show is the highest-rated, most embarrassing show on television!"

"I know," Belinda said, shrugging. "It really would just be easier for all concerned if you honored your agreement and answered a few questions about your crimes, your childhoods, what on Earth you were thinking when you decorated this house. . . ." She was looking at the painting over the fireplace, which was called *Unmarked Grave*.

Big Nana sighed. "Fine," she said, sounding defeated, like the French after the Battle of Waterloo. "You win. Why don't I show you around the Loot Cellar? It's where we keep all the fruits of our crimes. And the vegetables too."

"That's more like it!" said Belinda Smell, and she followed Big Nana out of the living room and down the staircase that led to the Loot Cellar.

Imogen followed Big Nana and the camera crew down to the Loot Cellar in the basement of Crim House. Big Nana typed in the combination lock on the disturbing-looking door, which was decorated to look like a gnome's face, and stood back as the door swung open. "After you . . . ," said Big Nana. "As a special treat, you can each keep one thing you find in the cellar." She winked at Imogen. Which was the Crim way of saying "Don't worry. I have a plan."

The camera crew walked into the Loot Cellar and looked around, saying things like, "Wow! A VHS copy of *Dirty Dancing: Havana Nights*!" and "Really? An ashtray shaped like a colon?" and "Help! It's the original Broadway cast of *Cats*! I have a phobia of full-body leotards!"

But no one helped them. Because Big Nana had already slammed the door in their panic-stricken faces.

She gave Imogen a high five. "Well, my overly sweet pumpkin spice latte," she said. "I think it's time for a family meeting."

Ten minutes later, the Crims were all crammed into the living room, waiting to hear what Big Nana had to say. The Horrible Children were sitting on the floor with Freddie and Imogen, throwing small knives at one another, and

Aunt Bets sat on the sofa, embroidering swear words onto pillows, next to Josephine, who was watching a YouTube video about contouring. Uncle Clyde stood in the doorway, doodling a new plan to steal the Victorian era from the past; Al was working on quadratic equations in a corner; and Uncle Knuckles was standing by the fireplace, reading a book called *Mindfulness and Murder: Making Peace with Your Pathological Past.*

"Right, my typhoid-flavored turnips," said Big Nana. "This meeting is going to be short and sweet, like an adorable child actress. I want each of you to pack an overnight bag. We're blowing town!"

"By which you mean we're leaving, right?" said Imogen. "Not destroying Blandington with a nuclear bomb or anything?" It was always best to clarify these things when Big Nana was involved.

"That's right, my bite-sized bran muffin," said Big Nana. "I need a vacation, anyway. And besides, we're totally out of uranium."

"WONDERFUL!" Uncle Knuckles shouted happily. "I KNOW THE PERFECT PLACE FOR A BIT OF REST AND RELAXATION!"

"We are not going to that yoga retreat you're so fond of," said Big Nana. "They serve only vegan food, and last time, you completely destroyed the teacher's chakras."

"I'M NOT TALKING ABOUT THE YOGA

RETREAT!" said Uncle Knuckles. "THE PLACE I'M THINKING OF IS MUCH MORE CHILLED OUT THAN THAT!"

Imogen sighed. She couldn't be sure what Uncle Knuckles's idea of a chilled-out vacation spot was. But if it was anything like his idea of a "gentle walk"—a two-week trek up Mount Kilimanjaro—or his signature "mild" curry, which contained several ounces of gunpowder, she wasn't going to find their vacation very relaxing at all.

IMOGEN HAD TO admit she'd been wrong about Uncle Knuckles's choice of vacation destination. She had been picturing something terrifying and dangerous, like a weeklong scuba diving expedition with an hour's worth of oxygen, or a weekend break in the murderers wing of a high-security prison. That, at least, would have been interesting. But it turned out, Uncle Knuckles's idea of a great place to stay was a four-person caravan in Dullport, Britain's least interesting and most rundown seaside resort.

Dullport had everything you wouldn't want in a vacation destination: a derelict pier complete with signs reading "Danger of Death"; fish and chip shops complete with signs reading "Danger of Death"; far too many rats, not counting Sam's pet ones; and an amazing lack of sunshine. The Crims had been there for a week now, and it had been raining ever since they had arrived. They knew the sea was out there somewhere, but they couldn't see it, what with all the fog and mist and hailstones that were in the way. Imogen was beginning to wish they'd gone to the yoga retreat. Even a room full of middle-aged women trying to contort themselves into the pigeon pose and talking about "living their best lives" would have been more entertaining than this.

"I DON'T UNDERSTAND!" shouted Knuckles, studying the Dullport brochure as the Horrible Children tried to kill one another with rocks. "IT'S SUNNY AND WARM IN ALL THE PICTURES."

"Ugh, hello?" said Delia, dodging a small but fast-moving pebble. "It's the middle of March, and the photos in that brochure were probably taken in August."

"DEFEATED BY THE SEASONS YET AGAIN!" cried Uncle Knuckles, shaking his massive fist, which, unbeknownst to him, sparked off a small tornado in Cambodia.

Imogen walked to the grimy window of the caravan and looked out at the nonexistent view. As she did so, a pigeon flew headfirst into the caravan and fell down dead with a thud. She didn't blame it. She felt as though she might go mad from caravan fever, which is a bit like cabin fever but much worse, because caravans have less effective ventilation than cabins, and the Crims had been eating a lot of fried fish. Plus, there was a donkey in the caravan, which Delia had "freed" from a donkey ride at the beach, "because animal rights," and which had taken over the only bedroom in the caravan, eaten the pillows, and was now vomiting them back up again all over Uncle Clyde's shoes.

"When can we admit that this was a terrible idea and go back home?" Imogen asked.

"When we're sure the crew is dead," said Big Nana, taking a bite of deep-fried cod.

"But that won't happen for ages," said Freddie, who was searching a cabinet for a jigsaw puzzle that wasn't missing all the exciting bits. "The Loot Cellar is actually very well stocked with food; Macaulay Culkin and his brother have started an organic vegetable business down there."

Freddie found a puzzle and shook out the pieces onto the floor. The Horrible Children started trying to put them together.

"All the pieces are white," said Delia.

"That's because the picture shows Dullport during a blizzard," said Freddie.

The twins started stabbing and cutting the pieces with knives (large, illegal ones) to make them fit, but that just made the whole thing seem even more pointless.

"What about some good old-fashioned entertainment?" asked Sam, in his new, deep voice. "We could form a barbershop quartet and sing close harmony together."

"THAT WOULD BE LOVELY!" said Uncle Knuckles. "I DO A GREAT VERSION OF CHRISTINA AGUILERA'S 'BEAUTIFUL.'" He closed his enormous eyes and started to sing. The noise was so appalling that it shattered the windows in the caravan. And then, to stop Uncle Knuckles's singing, Henry started to garrote him with the electrical wires, which caused the one working light in the caravan to sputter and die.

"We're all going to kill one another before we get home," Imogen said to Big Nana, who was now sitting on the sofa, reading a copy of *What Caravan?* magazine that she'd found in the bathroom. "Or is that the idea?"

"Stop complaining," said Big Nana, admiring a horse-drawn, two-bed caravan that cost seven guineas (the magazine was very out-of-date).

"We don't even have any Wi-Fi!" moaned Delia, trying and failing to look at Instagram on her phone. "There isn't even any phone signal!"

"BUT THERE IS A TELEVISION!" shouted Uncle Knuckles, turning it on.

Big Nana looked up from her magazine and smiled.

"That's the same TV model that we had when I was a young child snatcher."

"Yeah," grumbled Delia. "When, like, dinosaurs were walking the planet."

"Don't be silly," said Big Nana. "You know that dinosaurs and humans didn't coexist. We did have a pet dodo, though. Poor little Norbert." She shook her head sadly. "He didn't deserve to be made into a stew. My brothers were monsters. Everyone knows the best way to eat dodo is to roast it whole and serve it with gravy and roasted potatoes."

"SUCCESS!" shouted Uncle Knuckles. He had managed to turn on the television. Though there wasn't much to see; the screen was filled with gray squiggles.

"My favorite show!" said Uncle Clyde, rubbing his hands. "Did you know that the static you get when you turn on a television is actually an echo of the big bang?"

"Who knew the big bang was so *boring*," said Henry, who was graffitiing the donkey's back with a Sharpie.

"Right," said Imogen. "That's enough. Let's take the donkey back to the beach—"

"No!" said Delia. "Mavis doesn't want to go back there. Do you, Mavis?"

Mavis kicked Delia over.

"See? That's a no," said Delia, getting back to her feet.

"I don't usually kick people when I agree with them," Imogen pointed out.

Delia scowled at Imogen. "Do you know what Mavis gets paid for giving rides at the beach? Nothing! And she's still got all her student loans to pay!" She handed Imogen a PETA brochure, and even if Imogen had wanted to read it—which she definitely didn't—she couldn't, because Mavis snatched it out of her hand and chewed it into a pulp.

Imogen turned to Big Nana. "Please, can we go home?" she said. "Before Mavis eats us, too?"

Big Nana shook her head. "Absolutely not," she said. "We're getting back to our roots, spending time by the sea. Did you know that our ancestor Captain Glitterbeard was a famous pirate?"

Uncle Clyde looked up from the ant trap he was designing—he had heard that ants were able to support more than five thousand times their body weight, so he was planning to train them to shoplift things for him—and asked, "How come you've never mentioned Captain Glitterbeard before? You know I've always wanted to be a pirate. I'd look smashing in an eye patch."

"I *have* mentioned him," said Big Nana. "You were obviously just too busy coming up with pointless, impractical heists to listen. Everyone knows about Captain Glitterbeard. He stole a huge fortune and buried it on a tiny Caribbean island."

Aunt Bets looked up from the cushion cover she was embroidering with a picture of Uncle Knuckles's big toe (the most aesthetically appealing part of Uncle Knuckles). "How come we haven't ever tried to find the treasure before, then?" she asked.

Big Nana sighed. "Well," she said, "there are . . . complications."

"Yeah," said Delia. "Like the fact that you made it up? How convenient that you're telling us this when we can't access Google."

Big Nana looked hurt (though that might have been because Mavis was biting her shoulder). "Have I ever lied to you?" she asked.

"Oh, no," said Delia. "Except that one time, about that minor thing . . . What was it? Oh yeah—BEING DEAD."

Big Nana sighed again. "You don't have to believe me," she said. "I just thought you'd like to know." And she disappeared behind her ancient magazine.

Imogen looked at her grandmother. She was curious. Big Nana had a history of lying about important things like who she was and the fact that she hadn't drowned during an underwater submarine heist. Was it possible that the Crims really did have a pirate ancestor who had buried his fortune on a far-off island and then forgotten to tell anyone where it was? *Yes,* she thought. *That's just the sort of stupid thing a Crim would do.*

Imogen needed some air—the smell of donkey was pretty overpowering—so she stepped over Isabella, who was reading a copy of *War and Peace*, and opened the door of the caravan. As soon as she was outside, she took a deep breath. The sea air was refreshing, though it was raining so heavily she felt as though she were taking a shower. She hugged herself against the cold and walked through the campsite to the center of Dullport. *Maybe I'll be able to get a signal here. . . .* She walked through the streets, waving her phone around, and tried to Google "Captain Glitter-beard," but it didn't work.

Imogen sat down on a bench outside one of Dullport's many terrible fish and chip shops. There was a plaque on the back of the bench, dedicated to the memory of a woman named Maureen who had apparently lived in Dullport her entire life. *She probably died of boredom,* Imogen thought.

"Hey! Imogen!"

Imogen turned around. The Horrible Children were running down the street toward her, looking more horrible than usual in the rain.

"We've got a great idea," Sam said, when they had reached her.

"I suppose there's a first time for everything," Imogen said.

"An idea for a crime," said Henry, kicking what he

thought was an ice cream cone but turned out to be a pointy rock, and then howling in pain.

"What kind of crime?" Imogen asked.

The twins opened their mouths to answer, but Imogen stopped them.

"Actually, never mind," she said. "Whatever it is, it has to be better than staring at the rain, or listening to Mum talking about the rain, or spending any more time in the presence of that revolting donkey."

"Hey!" said Delia, pouting. "You can't talk about Mavis like that. Donkeys are people, too!"

"They're really not," said Imogen, standing up. "Right, then. Delia and I are in charge, seeing as we're the only ones capable of pulling off a crime more complicated than stealing a three-year-old's pick-n-mix. Where are we going?"

"To the beach!" said Sam, leading the way.

Dullport Beach was the sort of place you would never, ever choose to go, not even if someone offered you a choice between sitting there in a deck chair for half an hour or jumping headfirst into a vat of sewage. There was no sand. There weren't even any pebbles. Instead, there were jagged gray rocks, possibly made of asbestos or the charred remains of people who had spontaneously combusted after watching one too many *Punch and Judy* puppet shows.

Unsurprisingly—because *Punch and Judy* shows are terrible, and Dullport was full of terrible things—there was a *Punch and Judy* show taking place on the beach right at that moment.

If you've never seen a *Punch and Judy* show, then you're an extremely fortunate human being (assuming you're not a goat that has learned to read. If you are, congratulations!). They're the worst kind of shows there are. They always have the same "plot": a puppet named Punch picks up a stick and hits everything he can see, including his wife, Judy; a crocodile; some sausages; a policeman; and the devil. Big Nana was a big *Punch and Judy* fan—she loved the violence, the criminals getting away with murder, and the disturbing puppets.

Sam led Imogen and the Horrible Children to the red-and-white–striped *Punch and Judy* tent. "Sam, you steal the donation cup," said Delia. "The rest of us will sit in the audience and provide backup if needed."

"Wait," said Imogen, pulling Delia aside. "Theft isn't really Sam's strong point. He's more of a fraud sort of guy."

"But how's he ever going to learn to steal if we never let him try?" asked Delia.

"Let's just think the plan through a little more thoroughly before we begin," said Imogen.

Delia rolled her eyes. "You used to be way more spontaneous. You're no fun anymore!"

"I am fun!" said Imogen. "I just like to plan my fun!" And then she heard what she had just said and laughed. "Okay, fine," she said. "I'll be spontaneous."

Imogen sat down in the audience, between an old woman who was staring off into the distance, smiling—perhaps because she thought she was somewhere else—and a weeping toddler, who obviously knew exactly where he was.

While Punch was hitting the policeman with his massive stick, shouting, "That's the way to do it!" for no apparent reason, Sam ran up to the tent and snatched the donation cup.

Imogen put her head in her hands. Sam hadn't even *tried* to be subtle about it. He should have caused some kind of distraction so the puppeteer wouldn't notice or waited until the end of the show when the crowd was milling around—something, anything, other than just snatching the money in front of an actual audience. *Have I taught Sam nothing?* she thought. *Where is the artistry? The cunning? The skill?*

Unsurprisingly, the puppeteer was quite angry. He let out a great roar of rage and started chasing Sam through the audience, wielding a gigantic, very deadly looking stick—a massive version of the one the Punch puppet was holding.

Imogen groaned and watched as Sam ran through the

crowd, tripping over the old woman and dropping the donation cup onto her head.

"Such painful rain!" said the old woman as the coins fell over her.

Imogen caught Delia's eye and gave her an "I told you so" look. That was the last time she let Delia take the lead in anything. Except ballroom dancing lessons (Delia was very good at the fox-trot). Imogen stood up and raced after the puppeteer, who was still chasing Sam and now the other Horrible Children, down the beach.

"That's the way to do it!" shouted the puppeteer, swiping at Sam with his stick.

The audience cheered.

"What large puppets," said the old lady, staring at Sam and the puppeteer.

Sam was nearly at the campsite . . . but the puppeteer was close behind. And then, just as it looked as though Sam might get away, he slipped on an abandoned bag of chips and fell, sprawled, on the beach.

"Got you now," said the puppeteer, looming over Sam, raising his stick in the air.

But the other Horrible Children surrounded him.

"Let him go," said Imogen.

"Or what?" said the puppeteer, turning to look at her. "I have a stick. What have you got?"

"We've got Isabella," said Henry. "Isabella, get him!"

And before the puppeteer knew what was happening, Isabella had grabbed his ankle and was gnawing at it as though it were a particularly delicious biscotti.

"Owww!" cried the puppeteer, hobbling away, using his stick to support himself.

Sam patted Isabella on the head proudly. "That's the way to do it!" he said. Imogen closed her eyes and sighed. She wasn't sure how much longer she could survive this "vacation."

IMOGEN USHERED THE Horrible Children into the caravan and slammed the door.

"You're back!" Uncle Clyde said cheerfully as the Horrible Children squeezed onto the sofa, which was flatter and harder than it should have been, because Mavis had eaten all the stuffing.

"Unfortunately," grumbled Imogen.

"Buck up, Imogen!" said Uncle Clyde. "I've managed to pick up a station on the TV!" He turned the television on and stood back with a huge smile. The screen flickered to life (black-and-white life, but still . . .). A newsreader appeared, shuffling his papers. "And this just in: There are reports of a bombing at Krukingham Palace— Wait, is that a typo?"

But before the newsreader could say anything else, Josephine rushed over to the TV and changed the channel. "I can't bear listening to the news when I'm on vacation," she muttered, sitting back down on an armchair and spritzing herself with a perfume called Delusions.

"Wait! Change the channel back!" said Imogen, leaning forward. Had she just *imagined* the newsreader saying something about Krukingham Palace being bombed? Or had he meant "Buckingham" Palace? Either way, that was a news story she wanted to hear. But then Imogen forgot all about changing the channel. Because a voice-over announced the premiere of a new comedy special, and then Uncle Knuckles appeared on the screen and immediately banged his head on a low doorframe. Canned laughter played as he rubbed his head and said, "ARCHITECTURE HAS ALWAYS HAD IT IN FOR ME!"

As Imogen was reeling from the revelation that her uncle was apparently a slapstick comedy star, her mother appeared on the TV too, and posing in the doorway, winking at the camera. "Can you believe I have a daughter?" she said. "I know! I look so young! But it's true! She always wears sensible cardigans, which add ten years, so people think we're sisters." She batted her eyelashes.

Canned laughter played again. Real-life Josephine

frowned. "Hey," she said. "That wasn't supposed to be a punch line."

Imogen stared at the television, openmouthed in horror, as one by one, the Crims appeared on the screen. This was the show Josephine had signed them up for, and it was neither the gritty crime drama Belinda Smell had said it would be, nor the glossy reality show Josephine had hoped for. The whole thing had been edited to make the Crims look like bumbling idiots, which, to be fair, couldn't have been hard.

The TV crew had managed to film the whole Mega Deals heist. Imogen watched through her fingers as Sam accidentally called his math teacher instead of the Mega Deals store. When Mr. Fry picked up, a *wah-wah-waaaah* sound effect played, and Sam dropped the phone and said in his deep voice: "Why do I have him on speed dial?"

"That's going to be your catchphrase!" Josephine said happily, rubbing Sam's head.

In the next scene, the twins collapsed on the floor of the store. The booming shop clerk turned to the camera and said, "Let's see how quickly I can get them to crack!"

Imogen had never felt so humiliated. Not when she'd been thrown out of Lilyworth. Not even when Uncle Clyde had entered her into the Blandington Zoo talent show dressed as a squirrel, to distract the zookeepers while he stole a raccoon. (Her performance of "Squirrels Just Want to Have Fun" had actually gone down pretty well.)

How could she not have realized that the heist was a setup? Self-doubt flooded through her like water through a very leaky basement. She had lost her touch.

But the TV show wasn't over yet. The crew had picked up everything the Crims had said during the heist, and they kept every snarky thing that Imogen had said—things like "You idiots!" and "Is he even *more* incompetent now that his voice has broken?" and "Really, Isabella's chosen this moment to stop being a miniature psychopath?"—to make it look as though she were insulting her family, or that she thought she was smarter than them. They played clips from her cousins' one-on-one interviews, which didn't make Imogen feel any better. They had been edited to make the Horrible Children seem like the Delightful Children, which they obviously weren't or everyone would have called them that. Nick had said, "I look up to Imogen so much! Mainly because she's taller than me," and Delia had said, "I love spending time with my family. But I don't like *doing* time with my family." And Isabella had said, "I love clowns!" Which came a bit out of nowhere. The producers were trying to make Imogen look like the bad guy.

Am *I "the mean one"?* Imogen wondered. *What if I'm the villain of the family, instead of the heroine?* She frowned. She didn't mind looking like a villain to the rest of the world—that's what criminals were, after all. But within her own family, she'd always thought she was the *good* one.

And in the end, she just wanted the Crims to be their best. Was that villainy or just having standards?

The other Crims didn't seem to have a problem with the editing. They were all too busy laughing.

"This is my new favorite show!" chuckled Uncle Clyde. "It's even better than *Deadly Car Chases Involving Cattle*!"

"Look how great my hair looks on camera!" said Delia.

Only one person wasn't smiling as she watched the television: Big Nana. She was standing by the door of the caravan, her arms crossed. She glared at Imogen with a face like thunder. And it looked as though there might be lightning on the way.

And she's not happy about what I had to say, Imogen thought.

Imogen had to talk to her grandmother and try to make it all okay. She squeezed past Sam, who was trying to introduce Mavis to Doom the hedgehog (it's fair to say that the two weren't about to become lifelong friends), and walked over to Big Nana. "Outside?" she asked.

Big Nana nodded stiffly and opened the door.

It was freezing cold outside, but at least it didn't smell of donkey. Imogen and Big Nana sat on the caravan step. Imogen had expected Big Nana to tell her off, but she didn't say anything at all, which was much worse.

"I swear I was edited to look bad!" said Imogen.

Big Nana shook her head. "Never blame the edit," she said. "You must have said those things, or they wouldn't have the footage. And you know what I always say: 'Never be honest on camera or on any other kind of recording device. Except on podcasts. You should always be honest on podcasts.'"

"But did you see what a mess the others made of the heist? You can't blame me for being frustrated." She looked at Big Nana. "Can you?"

"I don't blame you," Big Nana said sadly. "But remember: Nothing is more important than family. Apart from dinosaurs."

"But that's just the point!" said Imogen, standing up. She was feeling angry and guilty now, which is the worst combination of emotions. "I love this family! Almost as much as I love *Tyrannosaurus rex*! And I'm sick of us being a joke." She sighed. "I just don't feel like the others are even *trying* to get better at crime. I'm not being challenged anymore."

Big Nana patted the step next to her, and Imogen sat down again. Big Nana put an arm around her. "This happens to all the greats," she said. "Robin Hood, the mafia, Ronald McDonald . . . They beat their enemies, and they start to get bored." She smiled at Imogen. "We beat the Kruks. That's a huge achievement! And it means we can live a peaceful life without being mauled by a tiger. I thought that's what you wanted. You can go back to writing essays about the Tudors and knowing things about test tubes, just like you did at Lilyworth Ladies' College."

"That is what I want," said Imogen. But it sounded like a question. And Lilyworth—where she'd ruled over the school until just a few months before—felt like a million years ago.

I'm a whole new person now, Imogen realized. *Maybe I want different things. Maybe I want to be pushed outside my comfort zone.*

"Maybe you need to spend some time thinking about how lucky you are," said Big Nana. "Here." She reached into her cardigan pocket and pulled out a small notebook. "I'm not getting anywhere with this gratitude journal," she said, passing it to Imogen. "You try it." She stood up with an "Oof" and went back into the caravan, leaving Imogen outside on her own.

Imogen opened the gratitude journal. Big Nana had only written one entry:

Things to be grateful for:

1. White bread
2. Bees
3. Chickens (they look like tiny dinosaurs)
4. Submachine guns
5. Potpourri
6. My family

But Imogen was finding it harder and harder to feel grateful for her family. And she definitely wasn't grateful for potpourri. It looked like breakfast cereal and smelled like old people. So, what *was* she grateful for?

Imogen knew she should be happy. And she knew she loved her family, really. But at the moment, she couldn't seem to be around them without wanting to smother them in their sleep. She had to make a change.

She took a deep breath. Big Nana would be furious with her for what she was about to do, but if she didn't get out of Dullport, Imogen would become even more bitter and mean. She had hated watching herself on the terrible TV show and hearing how horrible she was to her cousins. Big Nana was right—the camera crew hadn't invented the snarky things she had said. . . . *I want to be a villain,* Imogen thought. *But not at the expense of my own family. So I might as well team up with Ava and become a supervillain, instead of taking my villainy out on the people I love. . . .* She nodded to herself. This was for the benefit of her whole family. Just like the Crims Aid concert she had staged one Christmas, to trick people into giving money to them instead of to a real charity. *Plus, I really need a proper vacation,* she thought. *One that isn't in a place advertised as* Britain's Cheapest Seaside Resort . . . for a Reason*!*

Imogen tore a page out of the gratitude journal and scribbled a note to Big Nana. She didn't want anyone to think she'd been kidnapped, which would have been a reasonable assumption to make, seeing as the Kruks had recently managed to kidnap her entire family and force them to listen to the world's worst bedtime story in the presence of too many sharks. She slipped the note under the caravan door; she didn't risk going back inside, in case her mother forced her to appear in another terrible reality show, or Sam introduced her to one of his awful pets, or Henry set fire to her ponytail. She took out her phone again and walked along the beach in the rain, until she reached Dullport Pier. Maybe if she walked to the very end, she'd be able to get a signal. . . .

It worked! One bar! She texted Ava: **Hey, loser. You in the Caribbean yet? Can you swing by Dullport and pick me up? You'll know you're going the right way because all the fish will be swimming as fast as they can in the other direction.**

She sat down at the end of the pier, her legs dangling off the edge, waiting for Ava to reply. The sun started to go down. A lonely-looking clown came out of the arcade and started to tap dance. Imogen made a mental note to tell Isabella about it. At last, when Imogen wasn't sure how much longer she could watch a man in a red nose doing step-ball-changes, her phone buzzed with a message from Ava: **THOUGHT YOU'D NEVER ASK. SEE YOU IN TEN.**

IMOGEN DIDN'T HAVE to wait long for Ava. Exactly ten minutes after her text, Ava surfaced in a submarine. The Kruks might be mass murderers, but they were very punctual.

Imogen climbed aboard the submarine. She would never have admitted it to Ava (admitting things to Kruks often ended painfully), but she was quite disappointed. She wasn't going to get much of a suntan if she had to sunbathe indoors on a boat that traveled underwater. "I thought you said you'd stolen a cruise ship," she said.

"I said I was *going* to steal a cruise ship," said Ava,

handing Imogen a delicious, fruity drink with a cocktail umbrella in it. "But I need you to help me do it."

Imogen couldn't help feeling flattered. Someone needed her help with something other than cheating on their biology homework. "All right," she said. "Let's do it." It would be worth hanging out in another dark, damp vehicle for a while if it meant she'd feel like she was good at crime again.

But when Ava led Imogen into the submarine, it turned out it wasn't dark and damp at all. It was huge and luxurious—the most luxurious submarine Imogen had ever seen (and she'd seen a surprisingly large number of them. When she was younger, Big Nana had taken her along on training missions for the Underwater Submarine Heist). The boat looked as though it had been recently decorated by the world's best interior designer, which it had—Ava had kidnapped him from the World Interior Design championships, where he had won first prize. There were velvet sofas and ornamental fountains and a man-made beach with real sand and a hammock hanging over it.

The world's best interior designer was cowering by the hammock, wearing a very fetching lime-green tuxedo, holding a fabric swatch and a measuring tape. "Can I go now? Please?" he begged.

"Whatever," said Ava, waving her hand at him.

He climbed out of the hatch as fast as he could, tuxedo flapping, without looking back.

"I've been working my way up to the cruise ship, refining my boat-stealing technique," Ava said. "First I stole a dinghy, then a fishing boat, then a yacht, then a ferry. I'm getting better with each boat, if I do say so myself." She beckoned Imogen over to the hammock. "Here, try it out! There's a sensor on it, so as soon as you lie down, a UV light shines in your face and relaxing beach noises start playing."

Imogen lay back in the hammock and closed her eyes. She smiled as she felt the fake sun on her face, and heard the sound of fake waves and seagulls in her ears. She sipped a fruity drink and felt herself relax. As long as she didn't open her eyes, she could pretend she was really on vacation.

"You hang out and chill for a bit," said Ava. "I'll be back soon."

"No worries!" said Imogen, taking another sip of her drink. She was beginning to feel drowsy. The hammock was rocking gently, and the birds were singing softly, and the sun was shining on her artificially. . . .

Imogen jerked awake. How long had she been asleep for? And where had Ava gone?

"Ava?" Imogen called.

Nothing.

She hopped down from the hammock. The seagull noises stopped, and the sun disappeared. "Where are you?" called Imogen.

"Sorry!" said Ava, hurrying back into the cabin. "I was just . . . in the control room. This submarine doesn't steer itself, you know!"

But something about the way she said it stopped Imogen from believing her. Ava looked . . . suspicious. "Is there something you're not telling me?" asked Imogen.

"Fine," said Ava, holding her hands up. "I had some dodgy clams for dinner last night. Happy?"

That explains it, thought Imogen. *Diarrhea always makes people act suspiciously.* "Where is the rest of your family?" asked Imogen. "How come you didn't just get one of *them* to help you steal a cruise ship?"

Ava sat down on the hammock. "Would you want to go on vacation with any of my relatives?" she asked.

"Good point," said Imogen.

"Anyway," said Ava, "I was getting tired of them. They were holding me back—they kept threatening one another with machetes when we could have been stealing the gross national profit of Portugal and things like that."

"Same!" said Imogen, sitting down on the hammock next to Ava. "I am so over my family!" And she told Ava about the terrible TV show and the humiliating Mega

Deals heist and the donkey. Then Ava told her about the fingernail pulling and dismembering that went on in her family, and things didn't seem so bad.

"Listen, though," said Ava. "We don't have to be completely alone—we could help each other. Together, we could take over the world!" And with that, she threw her head back and gave an impressive evil laugh—so impressive that the hairs on Imogen's arms stood up, as if they were trying to get as far away from Ava as they could.

Imogen gave Ava and her laugh a round of applause.

"Thanks," said Ava, smoothing down her already very smooth hair (evil laughing tends to mess it up). She smiled at Imogen. "I trust you, as much as any supervillain can trust another supervillain."

Ava thinks I'm a supervillain? Imogen felt her face flush with pleasure at the compliment. These days, what with only being able to steal electronics because the store clerks were playing along, she felt like she barely even counted as a villain, let alone a supervillain. She smiled back at Ava, and said, "I trust you too." Which was true, sort of. Ava was much more reliable than her family . . . crime-wise, at least.

Imogen and Ava spent the rest of the morning planning the cruise ship takeover. Imogen felt like herself again—the best, most talented, least virtuous version of herself. She and Ava were the perfect team; Imogen was more of a details person, and Ava was good at the big picture. Literally, Imogen had never met anyone so good at drawing giant diagrams of crime scenes.

"First I'll hypnotize the captain," said Ava, drawing on a monogrammed whiteboard.

"With a watch?" asked Imogen.

"Exactly," said Ava. "I stole this one from my uncle." She took a gold pocket watch on a chain out of her pocket and dangled it in front of Imogen's eyes. "After I nicked it, I found out it was worth only a couple of million. So I might as well get some use out of it." Imogen felt her eyes closing. She was feeling sleepy. . . .

"Imogen," said Ava, snapping her fingers. "Wake up."

Imogen blinked. "You're good at that," she said.

Ava shrugged. "I'm good at everything."

Which reminded Imogen why she had hated Ava when she first arrived in Blandington. She tensed slightly, but then she shook off the jealous feeling. She and Ava were friends now, and no one was perfect.

After lunch (a delicious asparagus risotto), they practiced their evil monologues.

"Yours is missing a mustache-twirling moment," Ava said after Imogen had delivered hers.

"I don't have a mustache," said Imogen.

"You need to *imagine* you have one," said Ava.

"But everyone knows eyebrow twirling is the new mustache twirling," said Imogen, demonstrating.

"Interesting," said Ava, nodding. "Is that part of your personal brand?"

"I don't really have a personal brand," said Imogen. At least, she didn't *think* she had one, although the TV producer had labeled her as the family villain. . . . Maybe she ought to embrace that?

Ava looked horrified—as horrified as if Imogen had said, *I'm going to move to the suburbs and become a high school teacher.* "You've *got* to have a brand!" she said.

"Okay," said Imogen. "My personal brand is 'being a villain.'"

Ava rolled her eyes. "Well, duh," she said. "Of *course* you're a villain. But you need something that sets you apart from everyone else! Something memorable! And you need a good catchphrase, too. Staying on-brand is the essential skill of any supervillain! There are so many people committing crimes these days—if you want media coverage, you've got to have a unique selling point. Something that will make superheroes want to fight you, and other supervillains want to be you. Having a strong brand is the only way to make sure your name goes down in history!"

Imogen felt hot with humiliation. Of *course* every villain needed a brand. Why had she never thought of that?

No wonder the Crims were struggling. If they *did* have a brand, it was probably "world's most incompetent crime family." She felt as though Ava had found her out: She wasn't a supervillain after all. She was just a mediocre-villain.

Shake it off, Imogen, she told herself. She didn't believe in low self-confidence any more than she believed in Santa Claus or giving money to charity. She was Ava's equal. Except in terms of height and hair glossiness and the number of tiaras she owned. "Whatever," she said. "It's time to work on our disguises."

By late that afternoon, the plan was in place. Ava and Imogen put on their service personnel overalls and steered the submarine to a nearby, slightly less depressing seaside town called Mildlyinterestingport. They surfaced at the pier, where a huge cruise ship was being serviced.

Imogen and Ava climbed out of the submarine and stood on the pier, staring up at the cruise ship. Imogen's breath caught as she looked up at it. It was huge. Practically a skyscraper. There must have been thousands of people on board. How were she and Ava ever going to overpower them all? She was out of her depth, like Isabella in the shallow end of a swimming pool.

"First of all," said Ava, shielding her eyes against the sun and looking around. "We need to find the captain. . . ."

Finding the captain was easier than they had expected. They practically tripped over him as they walked along the pier: He was lying down on a towel in the sun with his captain's hat shading his eyes. He wasn't sunbathing so much as sunburning—his hat wasn't covering his nose, and it had turned a radioactive shade of pink.

Ava walked up to the captain and cleared her throat. "Hello," she said. "Lovely sunshine we're having, isn't it?"

Before he even opened his eyes, Ava whipped out her pocket watch, and she was swinging it back and forth in front of the captain's gaze. "You are feeling sleepy," Ava said, in her deep, hypnotizing voice.

"Sleepy," said the captain, his eyelids drooping.

"You are under my power," said Ava.

"I'm under your cow," said the captain.

"'Power' not 'cow,' you idiot!"

"Idiot," said the captain, nodding.

"Now," said Ava. "You're going to get back onto the ship and make an announcement. . . ."

Ten minutes later, Imogen and Ava were standing on the upper deck of the cruise ship, listening to the captain's voice crackle over the loudspeaker.

"Attention, crew, passengers, stowaways, and any pigeons hoping for a free holiday to Norway. I'm sorry to have to tell you that a rare digestive virus has been discovered on the ship—"

And just as Imogen had hoped they would, the passengers and crew members ran screaming from the ship as soon as they heard the words "rare," "digestive," and "virus."

Ava marched up to the captain, who was looking around, clearly wondering why his ship was empty, and waved her pocket watch in front of his eyes again. "Set sail for the Caribbean!" she said in her hypnotizing voice. "I hear Aruba is lovely this time of year."

The captain nodded, a glazed look in his eyes, and hoisted the anchor.

"How did you learn how to hypnotize people?" asked Imogen.

Ava shrugged. "Took an online course," she said. "The only side effect is that every time he hears the word 'and,' he'll think he's a chicken."

The captain immediately stopped sailing the ship and attempted to lay an egg.

"Darn," said Ava. "I should have thought that one through."

"You think they could have chosen a different word," said Imogen as they watched the captain preen his nonexistent feathers. "One that's less likely to come up in conversation. 'Onomatopoeia,' or something."

Ava shrugged again. "You get what you pay for," she said.

Once the captain realized he was human, they sailed out of the port into the open ocean. Imogen and Ava made themselves virgin daiquiris and settled into loungers on the top deck. The sun was shining, and Imogen felt good. She was committing a crime while taking a vacation. She had killed two birds with one stone (ducks—she was going to serve them with pancakes for dinner that night). Everything was going to plan.

And that's when her phone buzzed with a text from Big Nana.

Where are you, my small but delicious macaroon? Why did you leave? Come back!

Imogen felt guilty at first, but then she shrugged it off. Sure, she had disappeared without saying anything, but at least she'd left a note. Big Nana would find it eventually. And anyway, Big Nana had disappeared without saying anything and *pretended to be dead* for two years. Imogen didn't owe her anything.

"So," said Ava, "I say we spend the first few days in Aruba chilling out on the beach—"

"Hang on a sec," said Imogen. She stood up, walked to the railing at the edge of the boat, and threw her phone into the sea. It disappeared with a satisfying *splosh.* She settled back onto her lounger and took another sip of her drink. "You were saying?"

"We could steal a couple of surfboards," said Ava, "eat blue gelato just because it exists, listen to Justin Bieber. . . ."

Imogen sat up. "You actually *choose* to listen to Justin Bieber?"

"What?" said Ava. "He's got a great voice, and he's served time in jail! What's not to love?"

Imogen couldn't argue with that. She smiled and closed her eyes. She was experiencing an unfamiliar emotion—a strange lightness, a sense of contentment, that all was right with the world.

Was this what it felt like to be happy?

IMOGEN AND AVA got up early the next day to do all the things supervillains like to do on vacation: read books, go paddleboarding, and commit white-collar cybercrime. They needed money to fund their vacation—cruise liner fuel is horribly expensive—so after breakfast in the well-stocked cruise ship buffet, Imogen settled onto her favorite lounger and used one of the laptops they'd found in an office on the cruise ship to hack into a bank's database.

"Let's steal money from a corporation so rich that they won't even notice," said Ava, looking at the laptop screen over Imogen's shoulder.

"I know just the one," said Imogen, hacking into the WoosterLoo account.

Ava pulled a face. "Ew. A firm that makes portable toilets? Why?"

"No reason," said Imogen, as she started to siphon money from WoosterLoo into her bank account. WoosterLoo was the company owned by Jack Wooster, her uncle Clyde's number one enemy, who had tried to frame the Crims and send them to jail earlier this year.

They lay back and sipped their smoothies, watching the numbers in their account creep slowly upward.

"It's a pleasure doing business with you," said Ava. "We make a good team."

Imogen nodded. "We're practically Manchester United."

"Oh, no, we're better than *them*," said Ava. "Luka held them hostage a couple of months ago and forced them to play a five-a-side match against the Kruk soccer team."

"And the Kruks beat them?" Was there *nothing* the Kruks weren't world champions at?

"No," said Ava. "Manchester United won. But then Luka set the tigers on them, so now they've slipped down the league. It's hard to kick a ball when you're missing most of your . . ." Ava trailed off. She looked a little uncomfortable for some reason. Which was odd, because the loungers had memory foam cushions on them.

"What's the matter?" Imogen asked.

Ava looked around to make sure no one was listening, which was a bit unnecessary—the only other person on the ship was the captain, and he was currently pecking at some birdseed on the upper deck. "Come down to the movie theater," she said. "I've got something to tell you."

Imogen looked at Ava. "This ship has a movie theater?"

"Obviously," said Ava. "As if I'd bother stealing a cruise ship without one."

The movie theater was all gold leaf and red velvet seats. There was popcorn scattered in the aisles, and an old movie was paused on the screen—the passengers had obviously heard the captain's announcement and run out in the middle of the film. The whole place looked spooky, as though it might be haunted. Which it was. The ghost's name was Albert, and he particularly liked romantic comedies.

Ava found the remote control that operated the streaming device and turned the movie off. She and Imogen helped themselves to an abandoned tub of popcorn and sat down in the back row.

"Listen," Ava said.

"I can't hear anything," said Imogen.

"No, loser," said Ava. "Listen to *me*, I mean. I haven't been entirely honest with you."

"That's not surprising," said Imogen. "You *are* a supervillain."

Ava nodded. "It doesn't come naturally to me to trust people. Last time I trusted someone, my cousin Bernard threw me in the shark tank, and I lost a little toe. Our family plastic surgeon reattached it, so it wasn't a big deal, but you can see why I have issues." She smiled at Imogen. "I think you're nearly as good a supervillain as I am, though, so I'm going to try to trust you."

"Okay," said Imogen, wondering whether to argue about the "nearly as good" thing and deciding it would probably be best to let it go.

Ava ate a piece of popcorn. "I'm not just going to the Caribbean for a tropical vacation. Although that will certainly be a highlight." She dropped her voice to a whisper. "I'm really going to the Caribbean to destroy . . . *the Gull.*" She looked at Imogen, clearly waiting for a reaction, but Imogen wasn't sure what sort of reaction to give. Ava obviously really, really hated seabirds, which was understandable—they did have a tendency to steal your fries and poop on benches when you were about to sit on them—but going all the way to Aruba to kill a seagull when there were plenty in the UK seemed a little eccentric, even for someone who had once hijacked all the radio stations in Britain and forced them to play her brother's terrible rap song on repeat so that the rest of the country would hate him as much as she did.

"Is there one gull in particular that you have a problem with?" Imogen asked.

Ava looked horrified. "Do you seriously not know who the Gull is?"

Imogen shook her head. "Is that the new supercriminal from . . . Maine? Or something?"

"No!" said Ava. "The Gull is way worse than a rival supervillain. He's a super*hero*."

"Superheroes aren't real," said Imogen. "Are they?"

"They're not as common as the summer blockbusters would have you believe," said Ava, "but they do exist." She picked up the remote control and aimed it at the streaming device. "Here," she said. "Watch this."

She clicked around for a moment on a menu, then the cinema screen flickered to life, and a news report started playing.

"And this just in," said a bored-looking newsreader. "We're getting reports that Krukingham Palace, the underground headquarters of the Kruk crime family, has been destroyed. The superhero known as the Gull has claimed responsibility for planting the bomb. Law enforcement agencies worldwide were celebrating, as the location of Krukingham Palace had puzzled detectives for centuries. Police immediately swooped in: Two members of the Kruk family have been arrested, and more arrests are expected, as the Kruks seem to have no qualms whatsoever about informing on one another."

The video cut to Violet Kruk, giving a statement at a news conference, flanked by police. Imogen had always thought Violet was the most spoiled of all the Kruks—she liked to only wear clothes made out of endangered animals, and she ate Golden Grahams for breakfast (a cereal made out of men named Graham, who had been shrunk, freeze-dried, and coated in gold leaf). "My grandfather, the mass murderer Luka Kruk, is hiding out at 112 East Sheen Drive, Surrey," said Violet. "Feel free to arrest him. He bought me Ireland for my birthday, but it turns out it's not actually an Emerald Isle. The ground is made of grass, not precious stones! What a cheapskate! He does tend to eat police officers, though, so watch out for that. Also, my great-aunt Mabel murdered Marilyn Monroe and shot John F. Kennedy. And if anyone's wondering why red diamonds are so rare, it's because my sister, Lily, sticks them all over her body to pretend she's got measles when she wants to get out of swimming." She turned to the police officer next to her. "Is that enough? Will you let me go now? My pet Komodo dragon needs a manicure."

The bored-looking newsreader reappeared on the screen. "Most of the Kruks, however, did manage to get away, and there are no confirmed fatalities—though Don Vadrolga, who the Kruks were holding hostage, has not been seen or heard from since the attack. Which is odd, because they usually show *Retro Love* on the movie channels at least three times a day."

Imogen turned to Ava, who was eating popcorn and looking miserable at the same time, which is difficult, because popcorn is delicious. "Were you there, during the attack?" Imogen asked.

Ava shook her head. "I was in New York for the weekend, taking measurements of Central Park—we were thinking of modeling our back garden on it. Only ours was going to be bigger, obviously, with more helicopter pads." She sighed. "But now our whole house is essentially one big helicopter pad. Thanks to the Gull. *Now* can you see why I want to take him down?"

The news reporter was now talking about all the other criminals the Gull had brought to justice: the Russian mafia; the Italian Genovese family; the Killer Clan from the Philippines; the West London line dancing association. ("The Gull really hates country music," Ava explained.)

"Strange that he's never bothered the Crims," said Imogen.

Ava gave Imogen a pitying look. "You're not exactly A-list criminals, though, are you?"

Imogen was stung. But she had to admit that Ava had a point. How could the Gull take her family seriously when she herself couldn't? Maybe if the Crims branded themselves more cleverly, they would be big-time enough for the Gull to target. . . .

"So here's the plan," said Ava. "We're going to sail to the Gull's headquarters on his private island and attack while his attention is elsewhere. He's in South Africa at the moment, dealing with some very deadly wildebeests."

"Hang on," said Imogen. "The Gull has a private island?"

Ava shrugged. "Obviously," she said. "Every superhero needs a base. While he's away, we can sneak in there and take it over. We'll totally erase his DVR. He'll go nuts: It's the finale of *90 Day Fiancé* this week, and he never misses a show."

Imogen wasn't that impressed. "Is that it?" she asked.

"Well, no," said Ava. "Once he's back, of course, we'll turn his weapons against him and murder him. You have to make him miss his favorite show *first*, you see—it's called 'adding insult to injury.'"

Imogen nodded slowly. That was just Villainy 101. "And if we defeat the world's best superhero, that'll make us the world's baddest supervillains," she said slowly. "Which would definitely be a strong brand."

"Exactly!" said Ava, looking even more wild-eyed than usual. "So . . . are you in?"

"I am," said Imogen, after thinking for a minute. As Big Nana always said, "Never disappoint a wild-eyed Kruk, unless you're bored of having fingers."

"Great!" said Ava, and she went to hug Imogen, but she was still holding the remote control and ended up pressing one of the buttons, and the next thing they knew, Skype had loaded onto the big screen and they were in the middle of an eight-way call with several very famous supervillains.

Imogen stared at the screen, openmouthed. "Ferret Man is real?" she said. "And Bonnie and Clyde are still alive?"

"Sorry, guys! Wrong number!" Ava said to the supervillains, turning Skype off as quickly as she could.

"Why do you have all those mass murderers as contacts on Skype?" asked Imogen.

Ava looked at the floor. "Okay," she said. "Here's the thing. The thing is—"

"Just tell me the thing."

"I haven't been entirely honest with you."

Imogen laughed, without smiling. "You haven't even been *slightly* honest with me," she said.

"True," said Ava. "So, here's the deal. Those mass murderers are members of the International Association of Supercriminals. They are giving me strategic support to help me defeat the Gull—helping out with financing, acting as an IT help desk, that sort of thing. That's where I've been disappearing to. We have daily Skype meetings so I can update them on my progress."

Imogen frowned. "How come I've never even heard of the International Association of Supercriminals?" she asked. "Why haven't the Crims been asked to join?"

"Again," said Ava. "You're not A-list."

"Well, I can join you on the Skype calls from now on," said Imogen.

Ava made a face. "They're kind of selective about who they let in . . . ," she said.

Imogen felt crushed. Not as crushed as Uncle Knuckles had felt when he'd been trying to steal a skyscraper by pulling bricks out from the bottom, and the whole thing had fallen on top of him (he'd never been great at Jenga), but close.

"Look," said Ava, "I'll work on them. Okay? I know what you're capable of. . . ."

Imogen nodded. If the plot to bring down the Gull succeeded, it might improve the Crims' standing in the criminal underworld. Though that wouldn't be hard; Larry the mountain rescue dog had recently been sentenced to more time than the Crims had ever served. (It turned out that he had been embezzling money from the ranger station to feed his rawhide habit.) They'd brand themselves as the Gull Destroyers, and Imogen would be their supervillain in chief—a definite A-list criminal. Imogen allowed herself to fantasize about posing on the Felony Awards red carpet in a stolen Oscar de la Renta gown, accepting the prize for Best Break-In Artist, and thanking her parents for never reading to her as a child—but then her daydream was interrupted by an explosion from somewhere above them that shook the whole movie theater. Imogen sighed. All her best daydreams were interrupted by explosions or people stealing bits of her house.

"Keep low," whispered Ava. "And follow me." Crouching down, Ava and Imogen left the movie theater and ran up to the pool deck—and then they stopped running, because fireballs were flying through the air toward them like very flammable birds. One of them landed in the hot tub (which had been called the cold tub before the fireball landed in it).

"Is it the Gull?" Imogen asked, looking around to see who was attacking them. And then she saw where the fireballs were coming from, and she groaned. Because sailing alongside the cruise ship was a small, extremely homemade-looking pirate ship. Imogen looked closer—someone had taken a commuter ferry and rigged up an old-fashioned mast with sails made out of bedsheets. And at the very top of the mast was a hand-drawn pirate flag.

Down on deck, someone was aiming Molotov cocktails (the least delicious kind of cocktail) at the cruise ship with a slingshot. A very large person wearing an eye patch, a pirate hat, and a pink mohair sweater emblazoned with the words "I LOVE MY MUM."

"Uncle Knuckles," muttered Imogen.

"HELLO!" Uncle Knuckles said, waving before firing another Molotov cocktail in her direction.

But Uncle Knuckles wasn't alone. Of course he wasn't; one embarrassingly dressed uncle wouldn't have been humiliating enough.

"Avast, me hearties!" cried Uncle Clyde, popping up behind Uncle Knuckles. He was wearing a plastic eye patch, a polka-dot headscarf, and a frilly shirt that looked as though it had once belonged to an elderly lady named Doris. "Fearsome Captain Itchybritches will make ye walk the plank, ye scurvy scallywags!"

"I told you not to call me that," said Big Nana, walking out onto the deck of the commuter ferry. She was also dressed in a pirate costume—a faded headscarf, woolen breeches, a yellowing shirt that looked as though it probably smelled quite bad. Her costume was quite realistic, as though it might once have belonged to a pirate. A pirate who had been dead for a long time and hadn't been very keen on laundry when he'd been alive.

"But Captain Itchybritches suits ye," said Uncle Clyde.

To be fair, Big Nana's breeches did look pretty itchy.

Big Nana ignored him and turned to Imogen. "We've come to get you back," she said. "You know what I always say: You can't abandon the family in the middle of a vacation, unless you've been asked to appear at Coachella. And I don't think you have, have you, Imogen? So climb aboard."

BIG NANA REACHED her hand out to help Imogen climb from the cruise ship to the Crims' "pirate" ship, but Imogen didn't move.

"What are you waiting for?" asked Big Nana.

"For you to go away and leave me alone," snapped Imogen.

"That's not going to happen," said Big Nana, smiling very sweetly for a criminal mastermind. "So shall we do this the easy way? Or do I have to set fire to your hair?"

Imogen looked at Ava and shrugged. She didn't want to go back to her family, but she also really enjoyed not being bald.

But Ava shook her head. "I can't believe you'd give up that easily," she said. Then she pulled a small but extremely dangerous-looking cannon out of her pocket and then aimed it at Big Nana.

"Where did you get that?!" Imogen asked.

Ava rolled her eyes. "Dude, we're supervillains," she said. "Or at least, I am. You seriously think I'd travel without a cannon? There are a couple of cruise missiles downstairs, too, if you want to go and grab them."

But before Imogen could do anything, Al ran out onto the deck of the commuter ferry, dressed in a beautifully ironed frilly shirt, an eye patch, and a black pirate hat, and blasted a Molotov cocktail their way. He was a good shot, which was weird, as he'd never been keen on violence (except during Scrabble—"violence" is a very high-scoring word). "AVAST, YE LILY-LIVERED SCURVY DOGS!" he shouted, sounding very pirate-y.

"Dad," called Imogen, "what are you doing?" She felt a prickle of foreboding: The last time her father had been good at crime, he'd turned out not to be her father at all, but a Kruk wearing a very convincing prosthetic nose.

But Al didn't reply. Though to be fair, he probably hadn't heard her—Ava had just fired her cannon at him, and cannons are quite loud.

Al dodged the cannonball and dusted the gunpowder from his pirate hat, as if he did this sort of thing every day.

Which he didn't, although he was fond of playing battleships when balancing profit and loss statements got a bit much. He waved his cutlass in the air and cried, "Let the battle commence!"

Josephine rushed out on deck and flung herself at Al. She was wearing a bonnet and a white lace dress, and she was carrying what looked like a shepherd's crook. She obviously hadn't been able to bring herself to dress up as a pirate—the outfits weren't very glamorous—so was wearing a Little Bo Peep costume instead. "Oh, Al!" she said in a flirtatious voice that Imogen never wanted to hear again. "You're so *manly* when you're pretending to be a pirate! Never take that eye patch off!"

Al seemed to have taken charge of the battle. Imogen watched, amazed, as he handed cutlasses, daggers, and pistols to the other Crims and shouted orders at them in his most authoritative pirate voice. Imogen couldn't remember her father ever taking charge of anything before—not even the shopping list. (He had a tendency of buying things like tripe and lard that no sensible person ever wanted to eat, so Josephine wouldn't let him go to the supermarket.) "Dad," Imogen called, "when did you learn to be a pirate?"

Al shrugged modestly. "I was never any good at committing crimes on land, so Big Nana sent me to pirate summer camp when I was twelve. Best two months of my life. I learned to speak parrot; I stole thousands of pounds' worth of treasure; and I negotiated an excellent exchange rate on pieces of eight." He smiled sadly and shook his head. "Of course, there's not much cause for pirating skills in Blandington. I tried to sail my boat on the village pond once, but the neighbors complained it was too exciting."

"Al," said Big Nana, poking him with her dagger, "stop reminiscing about your glory days and get on with the raid!"

"Aye-aye," said Al, snapping back into his pirate captain character. "Hoist the mainsail!" he shouted to the twins, who were skulking near the dangerously homemade mast, dressed in matching sailor costumes (clearly there had been some misunderstandings at the costume shop).

"Aye-aye, Captain," they said.

"Get ready to stab Ava with your knitting needles!" he said to Aunt Bets, who was wearing what looked like a cabin boy's outfit, complete with ragged trousers and a headscarf, and was carrying it off surprisingly well.

"I'll dip the ends in poison first," she said happily, whipping the needles and her bottle of laudanum out of her sewing bag.

"Henry!" Al shouted. "Where are you? Come out here and sing Imogen and Ava your acoustic cover of that song with the 'Yo-ho-ho, and a bottle of rum'! That's enough to make anyone surrender."

Henry stumbled out onto the deck, feeling his way

with his hands— He was wearing an eye patch on each eye, which was taking stupidity to new heights, even for him. He grunted and cleared his throat.

"I'd anticipated this," said Ava, passing Imogen a pair of earplugs.

Imogen couldn't hear what Al said next because of the earplugs. He must have asked Sam to release his pet rats, because a moment later, Sam was on the deck, dressed in a lovely pair of stripy trousers, and the rats were scuttling toward the edge of the Crims' boat and hurling themselves into the water.

"Those rats are as stupid as the rest of my family," said Imogen, watching the rats splash around in the ocean.

"What?" said Ava, pulling out one of her earplugs.

But Imogen didn't reply, because her father had grabbed on to one of the ropes hanging from the pirate ship's mast and swung onto the deck of the cruise ship, legs swinging wildly, with an "ARRRRRGGGHHHHH!" that was oddly terrifying for a man whose idea of danger was doing equations without a calculator. He landed with a *plunk*, smoothed down his pirate costume, and pointed his cutlass at Ava and asked, "Would you care for a duel?"

"Not really," said Ava, pointing her cannon at him again.

"Wait!" said Imogen, jumping between her father and the cannon. Sure, her father was being much more irritating than usual, but she didn't really want him to be blown to pieces in front of her eyes. Or even behind her eyes. "I'll fight you," she said to Al.

"What with?" he asked.

"Good question," said Imogen. "You don't happen to have a sword on you, do you?" she asked Ava.

"Of course I do," said Ava, pulling one from her jacket pocket—she was like Mary Poppins, but with weapons.

Imogen took the sword and pointed it at her father. "I took fencing lessons at Lilyworth," she explained to Ava.

Al pointed his cutlass at Imogen. "En garde!" he shouted.

And they were off.

The Crims cheered and jeered and stroked their pirate beards while Imogen and Al swiped and parried and shouted "Touché!" at each other.

"Oh, Al," simpered Josephine, batting her false eyelashes. "You're so attractive when you're fighting our only daughter to the death!"

But Ava didn't seem impressed. "This is all very entertaining," she said, "but I hope you don't mind if I spice things up a bit." And she threw a grenade onto the Crims' ship.

The Crims shrieked and ran pointlessly about as flames spread across their ship.

"Help!" screamed Freddie "There's a fifty-fifty chance

the ship will sink before we have a chance to escape!"

Al looked over at the Crims, who were clearly waiting for him to tell them what to do.

"Please don't tell me I'm going to have to tell you what to do while I'm in the middle of a sword fight," said Al.

"Darling," said Josephine, climbing up the rigging to escape the fire, "you're going to have to tell us what to do, even though you're in the middle of a sword fight."

Al sighed. "Fine," he said, looking up as his sword clashed against Imogen's. "Nick and Nate, untie the rigging and swing across to the cruise ship."

"But it's really hard to climb the rigging with a peg leg on," said Nick.

"I CAN DO IT!" shouted Knuckles, scrambling up the knotted ropes, but halfway to the top, he looked down and started shaking. "I FORGOT THAT I'M SCARED OF HEIGHTS! MUMMY! CAN YOU HELP ME DOWN?"

"No," said Big Nana.

And then she ducked, because Ava was firing an anti-aircraft gun at the ship. (Ava should really have been shooting an anti-ship gun, but that was the one thing she didn't have in her arsenal.)

Delia ran out onto the deck, waving a pistol. She actually looked pretty good in her pirate costume—red trousers, a fake mustache, a very convincing hook. "Hey," she said, "you're not playing fair. We're trying to bring authentic pirate culture back. Real pirates kill one another at close range, instead of shooting at one another from a distance."

"Well, I'm part of the authentic *supervillain* culture," said Ava. "And we don't *care* about being fair. We care about destroying our enemies, by any means possible. And then eating their snacks. But if you really want to kill me in close quarters, be my guest. Come over here and fight me." She stopped firing and stood with her hands up. The pirate-y Crims looked at one another. "Come on," called Ava. "There are two of us, and, like, way too many of you. . . . Or is Al the only one brave enough to board our ship?"

"I BRAVE!" shouted Isabella, strolling to the edge of the deck and ripping off the huge inflatable straitjacket Uncle Clyde had dressed her in.

"No, darling—" called Josephine.

But it was too late. Isabella had already hurled herself over the side of the boat. Luckily, unlike Sam's rats—and the other Crims—Isabella could swim. She butterfly-stroked over to the cruise ship and hauled herself up its side with her freakishly strong nails and teeth. She plopped onto the deck . . . and clapped her hands. "What I do now?" she asked, looking at Al.

It wasn't really surprising that Isabella didn't have much

of an attack plan, seeing as she was three years old. And it wasn't really surprising that Ava *did* have a plan. She scooped Isabella up, tied her up with a rope, and plonked her in the middle of the deck.

"Right," she called across to the Crims. "Who's coming to rescue her?"

"Me!" shouted Freddie, swinging across to the cruise ship. But Ava was waiting for him. She caught him in a headlock as soon as he landed on the deck and tied him up with Isabella.

One by one, the other Crims swung across to try to save Isabella. And one by one, Ava tied them up. Even Big Nana—who tried to swing from the rigging and attack Ava from above—ended up bundled in between Henry and Delia. Soon, only Al was left, out of breath but still fighting Imogen. Imogen used all the tricks she was taught at school—the Korean defense, the Irish feint, the Belgian waffle distraction—and eventually, she managed to back her father into a corner until Ava could tie him up, too. He didn't seem to mind that much; he was still distracted by the waffle, which was cinnamon flavored.

Ava had tied all the Crims together with a pretty bow. She smiled at Imogen. "Pretty bows are part of my personal brand," she said, standing back to admire her handiwork.

Imogen, once again, felt humiliated to be a Crim. She

caught Big Nana's eye and mouthed, "What were you thinking?"

Big Nana looked hurt, though that was probably because Nick's cutlass was jabbing her in the back. "We had to get you back," she mouthed back.

Imogen felt guilty, and she didn't like feeling guilty, so she looked away and thought about Latin poetry until she felt bored instead.

Meanwhile, Ava prowled around the clump of Crims. "The question is, how will I kill you?" muttered Ava, twirling her eyebrows.

"Wait," said Imogen.

The Crims gasped. Imogen had broken Big Nana's cardinal rule: "Never interrupt a friend's evil monologue unless they're in danger of being eaten by a wild boar."

But Imogen ignored them. "You can't kill my family," she said.

"Yes I can," said Ava. "Have you seen the number of weapons I've got on this ship? Plus, I *want* to kill them. They'll just slow us down. And it's too late to take them back to Dullport now."

"Just put them back on the ferry!" Imogen pleaded.

Which is when the ferry exploded.

"Oh," said Imogen.

"It's for the best," said Ava. "The other Crims are like

oversized gnats. If we let them go, they'll just follow the cruise ship and keep attacking us until they get what they want."

Imogen looked around, desperately trying to find a way to save her family. "We can lock them in the hold," she said. "We can make them wait on us hand and foot. And face. And torso."

Ava waved her hand. "You're overcomplicating things. You know most criminals only get caught when they're stupid enough to leave their victims alive, right?" She patted Imogen's head, as if Imogen were a pony, or a dog, which she wasn't. "I've been waiting to give you something," she said. "Now seems as good a time as any. . . ." She reached into her pocket. Imogen flinched—so far, the only things Ava had pulled out of there had been weapons—and she was very relieved when Ava held out a bracelet with beads that spelled out "WWASVD?"

"It stands for 'What Would a Super Villain Do?'" Ava explained as she tied it around Imogen's wrist. "If you really want to achieve your full criminal potential, you have you ask yourself this question, over and over again. And then act on the answer."

"I'm not sure even a supervillain would allow their best friend to murder every single member of their family, though," said Imogen.

"Hey," said Delia. "I thought *I* was your best friend?"

Imogen ignored her. She didn't have time for Delia's jealousy. She looked at Ava and asked, "How would you feel if I killed all the Kruks?"

"That's so sweet!" said Ava, giving Imogen a patronizing hug. "As if you could! Look—go and have a piña colada or something. I'll take care of this."

"No thanks," said Imogen. "We're out of paper umbrellas, and everyone knows they're the best part. The point is, I know my family better than anyone. If you're really going to kill them, I should be there. To . . . help." *I have to come up with something,* she thought desperately. *If my family gets killed trying to "save" me from Ava, it will be my fault. . . . Maybe I* don't *have what it takes to be a supervillain. . . .*

Ava shrugged. "Okay," she said. "But this might be hard to watch." She clapped her hands. "Right, guys. Seeing as you're so keen on authentic pirate culture, I'm going to give you all an authentic pirate death. You're going to walk the plank."

"Hooray!" shouted Uncle Clyde. "I've always wanted to do that!"

"You can't swim, you great big unripe mango," pointed out Big Nana.

"That's a good point," said Uncle Clyde, starting to look appropriately, i.e., extremely, worried.

The other Crims looked worried too. Aunt Bets was biting her nails. Isabella was biting Delia. Imogen tried to hide how worried she was by smiling and saying, "Right, then! What are we going to use as a plank?"

Ava fetched a surfboard from the onboard sports equipment store and strapped it to the edge of the cruise ship with a piece of rope. Imogen peered over the edge of the boat as Ava worked. They weren't that high above the water . . . but everything's high when you can't swim. . . .

"You first," said Ava, pointing to Uncle Clyde.

Uncle Clyde edged his way along the surfboard, which wobbled precariously as he walked along it. Imogen said a silent prayer to the universe as he reached the end. He closed his eyes and said, "Life, it's been real," and stepped off into the sea.

It took a while for the splash to come. When it did, everyone looked over the edge. Uncle Clyde had disappeared . . .

And then bobbed to the surface, as if he were inflatable, which he was, sort of. He had taken off his ridiculous pirate shirt, and underneath, he was wearing a blow-up swimming costume. He looked a little disappointed. "So those weren't my last words?" he asked.

"You should be grateful they weren't," said Imogen. "They were terrible."

Ava gave a nasty laugh. "I hope the rest of you aren't planning to pull a stunt like that," she said.

The Crims looked at one another. They had, of course,

been planning to pull exactly the same stunt—originality wasn't a Crim strong point—so Ava patted them all down and confiscated the rubber ring that Delia had been hiding under her pirate skirt, and the water wings that Nick and Nate had concealed beneath their silly balloon sleeves, and the buoy that Sam was keeping under his hat.

"Oh buoy," he said as he handed it to Ava.

"I'm looking forward to killing all of you," Ava mused. "Not only will there be one less criminal family in the world, but there won't be nearly so many terrible puns." She pointed at Aunt Bets. "You next," she said.

"All right, dear," said Aunt Bets, picking up her handbag and smoothing down her wiry gray hair. Imogen felt a pang of affection for her, which was odd, because the pangs Aunt Bets usually caused were hunger pangs (she had a tendency of locking the Horrible Children in the cellar when they were being particularly annoying or flammable, feeding them only bread and water). Aunt Bets looked very old and very vulnerable as she wobbled her way to the end of the surfboard. She blew her family a kiss as she reached the end. "I love you all," she said. "Well. Most of you." And then she plunged into the ocean.

Aunt Bets took longer to bob to the surface than Uncle Clyde had. And as soon as she did, all her sweet-old-lady vulnerability disappeared, and she turned back into the psychopath they knew and loved. She swam over to Uncle

Clyde and tried to rip his inflatable swimming costume off him.

"Give it to me!" she shouted.

"No!" he shouted back.

"I'm too young to die!" she yelled.

"That is definitely not true!" cried Uncle Clyde. He looked up at Imogen and Ava and shouted, "Please! Take pity on me! This is a terrible way to die! I've always had nightmares about Bets drowning me. Please don't make them come true!"

Imogen glanced at Big Nana, who widened her eyes, as if to say "Do something!"

Imogen widened her eyes back, as if to say "Got any ideas?"

Big Nana widened her eyes even more—so wide that Imogen was slightly concerned her eyeballs might fall out—but Imogen couldn't understand what she was trying to say. Her eyeball interpretation skills weren't that good.

Ava pointed to Big Nana. "Captain Itchybritches," she said. "It's your turn to walk the plank."

Imogen's chest tightened. Once again, it looked as though she were about to lose her grandmother. The one consolation was that Big Nana didn't look that scared. She just looked slightly irritated. She stepped confidently onto the plank, as if she did this sort of thing all the time. And as she started walking to the end of the surfboard, Imogen had an idea.

She leaned against the railing at the edge of the cruise ship—attempting to look casual—and said, "It's a real shame we're killing all the Crims. Now, no one will find the priceless treasure that our ancestor Captain Glitter-beard buried on that private island. . . ."

Big Nana turned back to look at her, widening her eyes again. Imogen knew what she was trying to say this time: "Well done."

Ava turned to Imogen. "What?" she said.

"Yeah," Imogen continued. "Whatever the treasure is, it's meant to be truly, insanely valuable—the kind of fortune no one can assemble anymore, because of taxes and laws against turning elephants into necklaces, and things like that."

"I've always wanted an elephant necklace," said Ava.

"I know, right?" said Imogen. "And only Big Nana knows where the treasure is hidden. And how you compress an entire elephant into a tiny pendant . . ."

"That's right!" said Big Nana, teetering on the edge of the surfboard. "I've got a treasure map and everything. I'd be happy to tell you all about it . . . but first I'll need to fish my relatives out of the sea."

THE CRIMS ALL held their breaths, waiting to her what Ava would say. And then they stopped holding their breaths, because, as you yourself may have found out, humans need oxygen.

Ava crossed her arms. "Fine," she said. She stomped over to the cruise ship's sports equipment store again (it was extremely well stocked) and came back holding a huge fishing net. She fished the Crims out of the water, one by one.

"Want a hand?" Imogen asked her.

"No, I've got it," said Ava, dropping a very wet Uncle Clyde onto the deck. "Elsa used to make me practice weightlifting with white rhinos. Everyone thinks they're basically extinct, but there are, like, twenty living in the gym at Krukingham Palace. Except that just got bombed, didn't it? So they probably are extinct now." She plunged the net back into the ocean and heaved Aunt Bets onto the ship. Aunt Bets was clutching a couple of haddock that she had caught with her bare hands.

"In case we get hungry later," she explained.

Ava opened the door to the cruise ship's cabaret theater and marched all the Crims inside. "You're staying here," she said. "And don't even *think* about putting together a song and dance routine to the *Chicago* soundtrack to entertain yourselves. I find jazz hands very triggering." She slammed the door and locked them in.

Out on the deck, Ava raised one eyebrow at Imogen (all supervillains raise one eyebrow at least twice a day). "Are you serious about finding this treasure?" she asked. "I mean, obviously we have to defeat the Gull, but we could take a detour, if Captain Glitterbeard's hoard is really that valuable. . . ." She frowned. "But if it is, how come you're only just mentioning it now?"

Imogen shrugged. "You're so rich already," she said. "Your family invented diamonds. You get royalties every time someone types the letter *K*. I didn't think you'd be interested. But I guess you can never have too much treasure. . . ."

Ava laughed. "Tell that to my great-uncle Fernando Kruk. He drowned in a vat of liquid gold after melting down the crown jewels from seventy European countries."

"I don't think there are seventy European countries," said Imogen.

"There were, until Luka stole twenty of them and turned them into golf courses."

Imogen shuddered (subtly, so Ava wouldn't notice). She had forgotten how brilliantly evil the Kruks were. Imogen knew that Ava would want to kill her family eventually; if Captain Glitterbeard's treasure didn't exist, she'd murder them to punish Imogen. But if the treasure *did* exist, she'd murder them anyway, so that they wouldn't get in the way of her plan to confront the Gull. Imogen would just have to cross that extremely unpleasant bridge when she came to it. . . .

"So," said Ava, "what shall we do with your weirdo relatives once we've found the treasure? We don't want them messing up my plan to confront the Gull." It was as if she could read Imogen's mind. Perhaps she could; mind-reading technology was just the sort of thing the Kruks would develop to entertain themselves on a boring Sunday afternoon.

Imogen beckoned Ava away from the cabaret theater so that the Crims wouldn't be able to hear her and said,

"Maybe we could maroon them on the island where the treasure is. Then we could go and attack the Gull, save the world from justice, and pick them up afterward."

Ava didn't seem that keen on the idea. In fact, she said there was "no way in hell" she was going to "waste any of her time" on "third-rate criminals who couldn't pick a pocket even if the pocket jumped around waving it's nonexistent arms, screaming 'Pick me! Pick me!'" But privately, Imogen reasoned that as long as the Crims were still alive—which they would be, as long as Aunt Bets didn't start eating the little ones (always a danger)—then she could pick them up later without Ava.

"Let's go and ask Big Nana where the treasure is," Imogen said.

"I'll get the thumb screws," said Ava.

They opened the door to the cabaret theater and then shut it again straightaway, because there were horrible wailing noises coming from inside—noises that turned out to be Uncle Knuckles attempting to sing "Hello" on the karaoke machine. The noise he was making was so bad that the karaoke machine had spontaneously combusted, but unfortunately, that hadn't stopped him from singing. The other Crims were sitting on the floor, rocking and weeping, their hands over their ears. The noise was so bad that birds within earshot dropped out of the sky, dead.

Far away in London, Adele woke up shuddering, suddenly regretting that she had ever recorded the song. It was terrible.

Imogen and Ava stood in the corridor outside the cabaret theater, their hands over their ears, trying not to succumb to panic attacks.

"We've got to go back in there and save the others," said Imogen.

"I think my ears might explode if we do," said Ava. "And I like my ears a lot more than I like your family."

"Fine," said Imogen. "You stay here." She took a deep breath and ran back into the cabaret theater. One by one, she pulled the traumatized Crims out of the room. But even after she had dragged Uncle Knuckles onto the deck—and gagged him so that he'd never be able to sing anything ever again—she could still hear someone wailing, "Hello . . . it's me. . . ."

"Can you hear that?" she asked Ava.

Ava nodded. "Those lyrics will probably be burned into our brains forever."

But the song didn't sound quite as bad as it had when Uncle Knuckles had been singing it. "Wait," said Imogen. "I think someone *else* is singing a karaoke version of 'Hello' . . ."

"Why would they do that?!" wailed Ava.

"Why do good people die?" Imogen shrugged. "Why

do I always spill food all over myself when I'm wearing a white T-shirt?"

Ava cocked her head, listening to the singing. "It's coming from downstairs somewhere," she said. "I wonder if there's another deck down there. . . ."

"There's only one way to find out," said Imogen.

Ava nodded again. "By sending Isabella on a reconnaissance mission and hoping she makes it back alive."

"No!" said Imogen. "We go down ourselves! Supervillains never let their sidekicks do the dirty work."

"Not true," said Ava. "Supervillain sidekicks are always cleaning out litter boxes and doing the laundry. But I get your point."

Imogen and Ava left the Crims in a gibbering heap on the deck and went downstairs to find out where the noise was coming from. They passed the dining room and the captain's cabin, which was full of Justin Bieber memorabilia.

"It's getting louder," said Imogen. She pointed to a spiral staircase. "Maybe it's coming from the next floor down. . . ."

The staircase led to a ballroom complete with flashing disco lights and another karaoke machine.

And about fifty cruise ship passengers.

Most of them had gray hair and sensible shoes, and almost all of them were wearing either a sun visor or a

Hawaiian shirt. They seemed to be having a great time.

Imogen and Ava stared at the passengers. Then they turned and stared at each other.

"What is going on?" said Ava.

It was very clear to Imogen what was going on. The passengers were all dancing (at least they were waving their elbows and stamping their feet, so she assumed they were trying to dance) and singing along to the song Imogen now hated most in the world. (Which is saying something, because Henry had once written a heavy metal tune called "Imogen Smells Like a Pond." And if you'd ever smelled the pond at the back of Crim House, you'd know just how insulting that was.) But *why* this was going on was another matter. What were the elderly people still doing on the ship?

One of the cruise passengers—a nice, ordinary woman whom Imogen would later learn was named Barbara, who liked taking photographs of her grandchildren and watching puppies doing tricks on television, and who definitely didn't deserve to be trapped on a ship with a collection of criminals—said: "Oh, have you come to tell us it's dinnertime? The announcement system isn't working on our deck."

"So you didn't hear the captain's message?" Imogen asked.

"Oh, no, dearie," said Barbara. "What announcement? Do you know how long it'll be before we get to Norway? I can't wait to see the fjords!"

Ava looked at Imogen. Imogen looked at Ava.

"Oh dear," said Imogen.

"I'd have put it more strongly myself," said Ava, "but yes."

YOU KNOW THE way you get used to terrible things? Maybe you fall out with a friend, or do badly in an exam, or accidentally hijack a ship full of sweet retired people who believe they're going to Scandinavia, and you think the world will come crashing down around you, but it just carries on as usual?

That's how Imogen felt over the next few days. The cruise ship passengers hadn't noticed that anything odd was going on, possibly because they were mostly over the age of seventy and suffering from hearing loss/poor eyesight/the belief that everything on a cruise ship happens for a reason, even bad magicians and seasickness.

The Crims had taken over the running of the cruise ship and were actually quite skilled at hospitality. Aunt Bets wasn't great at customer service, sure, but she did make very good toast. Uncle Knuckles had volunteered to sing karaoke in the cabaret theater, but the other Crims all burst into tears at the very idea of hearing Knuckles sing again, so he agreed to deliver room service orders instead. The cabaret theater job went to Sam, who had a lovely baritone. He'd found a tuxedo in one of the abandoned cabins and entertained the guests three times a day with tap-dancing routines and songs such as "Cellblock Tango" and "Defying Depravity." And Freddie had started up his secret poker ring again, except this time it wasn't secret, because he kept announcing the games over the ship's loudspeaker. So far, he had won the entire lifesavings of three passengers, who now spent all their time in the bar area, crying. Imogen reminded Freddie to go easy on the poker players; they didn't need anyone being forced to punch himself in the face and losing all his teeth, à la Freddie's most indebted player, Unfortunate Pete. But in turn, Freddie reminded Imogen that cruise passengers have more money to burn than retired garbage men who hang out in the Tesco parking lot.

"Is that where you found your players?" Imogen asked.

"It's where I *used to* find my players," Freddie replied, pulling out a roll of very crisp euro bills. "Honestly, I should have been working the travel and leisure set all along."

A couple of days after the karaoke incident, Imogen and Ava were at the breakfast buffet, spooning cold scrambled eggs onto their plates and filling their pockets with yogurts and oranges, when Delia walked in.

Imogen waved her over. "Come sit with us!" she said.

Ava elbowed Imogen, the universal sign for "I don't want her to sit with us. She's not very good at white-collar crime." But Imogen ignored her. She wasn't going to let Ava call all the shots in their friendship. Just most of them.

Delia picked up a croissant and a cup of instant coffee and followed Ava and Imogen to a table near the pool. "You know we don't have to steal the yogurts," she said. "We've already stolen, like, the whole ship."

"Correction," said Ava, flicking her annoyingly shiny hair. "*We* stole the ship. *You* got in the way. And anyhow, your aunt Bets is weirdly uptight about people taking too much food. . . ." She nodded over to Aunt Bets, who at that moment was slapping the hand of a tourist named Kevin, who had helped himself to three sausages, and saying, "You've got to get used to small portion sizes if you're going to Norway. Eating too much makes you vulnerable to reindeer attacks."

"I didn't know that," said Kevin, happily handing back his third sausage. "I don't think I've ever been on such an educational cruise!"

"So," Imogen said, once she'd finished her scrambled eggs, "what do you guys want to do today?" She looked from Ava to Delia and back again; maybe if she just ignored the fact that they hated each other, they'd forget they hated each other too, and they could have steal-overs together (like a sleepover, except that when your friends have fallen asleep, you take their jewelry).

"Stop trying to make this friendship happen," said Ava, rolling her eyes and flicking her hair.

"Yeah," said Delia, rolling her eyes and flicking her hair, in an uncanny imitation of Ava. "My personal brand is being really shallow and self-obsessed and not having any friends except the people I pay to be around me."

Ava looked at Delia, interested for a moment. "Is it?" she said. "I didn't know you had a personal brand."

"I'm pretending to be you, you big, shiny idiot," said Delia.

Imogen had to physically restrain Ava from attacking Delia with her Swarovski crystal–encrusted penknife. Luckily, she'd had lots of practice preventing murders.

"Just you wait—" said Ava. But just then, the dining room door swung open, and Big Nana walked up to them.

"Lovely to see you all playing together nicely," she said, smiling her comforting yet disturbing smile.

Imogen, who was still holding Ava and Delia apart, said, "Can I trust you two not to kill each other till I get back? I need to talk to Big Nana about something."

"No," said Ava and Delia at the same time.

"But I do want to go and watch Sam's ten a.m. performance," said Delia. "He's taking requests, and I want to hear what he can do with Kitty Penguin's latest album. Also, I'm going to request that he stops adopting feral animals as pets. You know he has nine cockroaches now, named after the Supreme Court judges?"

"Fine," said Imogen, letting go of Delia and Ava.

Ava made "you're dead" motions to Delia as she left the room.

Imogen walked up to Big Nana and pulled her aside. "Listen," she said, looking around to make sure Ava couldn't overhear. "Does Captain Glitterbeard's treasure really exist? Because if it doesn't, things are going to get sticky. And by sticky, I mean dangerous. And by dangerous, I mean someone is going to take us all out the back and kill us, possibly with a cocktail umbrella. And by someone, I mean Ava."

Big Nana looked at Imogen. Her eyes were clear and blue, like honest paddling pools. "I wouldn't lie to you about something this important," she said.

"But I don't understand why you didn't tell us about the treasure sooner," Imogen said. "We always need money for things like leg reattachment operations and bail money and tins of Scotch broth soup—"

"The Crims do get through a surprising amount of Scotch broth." Big Nana nodded. She took Imogen's hand and patted it. "I never mentioned it because I never thought we'd get to the Caribbean," she said. "We can barely all make it to the newsstand and back without someone being arrested. And of course I don't actually know how much the treasure is worth. But Glitterbeard was a much more fearsome pirate than his brothers Ordinarybeard and Cant-growabeard. So it's probably worth quite a lot. . . ."

Imogen looked at Big Nana. Despite everything, she believed her. And because she believed her, she started to feel a bit guilty for promising the treasure to Ava and arranging for her family to be marooned on an island. But at least she'd managed to keep her family alive . . . so far . . .

Imogen didn't have time to feel guilty for long, because moments later, Nick and Nate came pelting down the stairs, calling out to her and Ava.

"There's another ship out there!" yelled Nick, pointing out to sea.

"Well, that's to be expected," said Imogen. "It *is* the ocean."

"No," said Nate, trying to get his breath back. "There's another pirate ship. The *Golden Bounty*!"

"And if its name is anything to go by, it'll be full of treasure," said Nick.

"Yeah, but your grandmother's called Big Nana, and she's only, like, five foot two," said Ava, sauntering over, her hands in her pockets.

But Nick and Nate weren't listening. "It's time for a proper pirate attack!" said Nate. "Entertaining the passengers is so *boring.* They keep tipping me. It's no fun being given money, instead of stealing it."

Ava shook her shiny head and crossed her shiny arms (she had just moisturized). "Absolutely not," she said. "We have to lie low. We don't want to attract any . . . undue attention from—"

Imogen had a feeling the end of the sentence was going to be "the Gull." But Ava never finished the sentence. Because that's when they heard cannon fire coming from the upper deck.

They ran upstairs. The Crims—dressed, luckily, in their awful pirate outfits—had launched a full-scale attack on the *Golden Bounty.* Delia was manning the cannon, barking orders to everyone like a bossy dog.

"What does she think she's *doing*?" said Imogen.

"She must have a death wish," said Ava. "Oh well. I like making people's wishes come true."

The attack was going just as well as the attack on the cruise ship had gone, i.e., not well at all. The crew of the *Golden Bounty* were standing on the deck of their ship, bemused, while the Crims ran around waving cutlasses and setting fire to things that shouldn't be set fire to. But at least the tourists were enjoying themselves. Imogen could hear them whooping and cheering from the deck below.

"The brochure didn't say there'd be such great entertainment!" said Kevin.

"This is way better than bingo!" said Barbara.

Once again, Al was the only Crim who seemed to have a clue what he was doing. He shouted to the captain to steer the cruise ship toward the *Golden Bounty*, but the captain was still making clucking noises and flapping his nonexistent wings. So Al raced up to the control room, his frilly shirt flapping in the wind, and grabbed the steering wheel.

"Starboard," Al yelled piratically as the cruise ship turned toward the *Golden Bounty*. He pulled them alongside the other ship and yelled, "Delia, keep firing that cannon! Henry, fetch the gunpowder! Clyde, Nick, and Nate, swarm the deck!"

Uncle Clyde, Sam, and the twins took his order a bit

too literally. They did jump aboard the *Golden Bounty*, but they pretended to be bees while they did it. The tourists whooped and cheered again as the Crims buzzed about the deck.

"Ugh," said Delia, shaking her head. "Families can be so embarrassing sometimes."

"I love interactive theater," Barbara said to a man named Jeremy, a retired carpenter who was really excited about seeing Norway's famous wooden churches. "I once saw a production of *Hamlet* in a public toilet. But this is even more exciting! Pirates who are also bees? Only a genius or an insane person could come up with something like that!"

"She doesn't know how right she is," said Imogen, watching Uncle Clyde pretending to sting the captain of the *Golden Bounty*, a more than usually insane gleam in his eyes.

Imogen shook her head. "That doesn't look like a pirate ship. It's probably a cargo ship. I bet it's full of goldfish. Or corn. Or— What else is golden?"

"Gold!" screamed Uncle Clyde.

"You idiots!" Ava screamed authoritatively. "No way is that ship transporting gold. It doesn't have good enough security! It's probably full of sewage or something! Get back here!"

But the Crims were very good at ignoring authority figures.

"Seriously!" Ava shouted. "You're all going to regret this more than people with lactose intolerance regret eating ice cream!"

"Food intolerances are a myth!" said Big Nana.

"I HATE TO DISAGREE," shouted Uncle Knuckles, holding his sword to the neck of the *Golden Bounty*'s captain, "BUT HAVE YOU SEEN WHAT HAPPENS TO ME WHEN I EAT LENTILS?"

"I've *smelled* what happens to him," said Aunt Bets. "And it isn't pleasant."

Imogen looked down at the *Golden Bounty* from the cruise ship. If she could have died of embarrassment, she would have. Her mad uncle and her equally mad cousins were still pretending to be insects. Sam had found the ship's cat and seemed to be having an actual conversation with it. A one-way conversation, sure, but that didn't seem to bother Sam. Henry had found some gunpowder, but had succeeded in only blowing his own pirate hat off his head. And Uncle Knuckles, who was at least holding the captain hostage, kept saying things like "THIS DOESN'T HURT TOO MUCH, DOES IT?" and "THOSE ARE LOVELY SHOES. WHERE DID YOU GET THEM?"

At what felt like very long last, Al and Big Nana pulled

themselves together and rounded up the rest of the *Golden Bounty* crew at gunpoint. The crew actually looked a bit relieved—at least they understood what was happening now.

"Hand over your treasure!" growled Big Nana.

"If this large gentleman would let me go and stop shouting in my ear, I'd be happy to," said the captain.

"OKAY!" Uncle Knuckles said as quietly as an extremely loud pneumatic drill.

Imogen held her breath. The captain was walking over to the hold and unlocking the door. . . . Had the Crims' attack actually worked? Maybe the *Golden Bounty was* a pirate ship! They did have a cat, and everyone knows that pirates love cats, almost as much as they love taking things that don't belong to them and singing songs about rum.

The captain rummaged around in the hold and pulled something out. He handed it to Henry.

"What's this?" said Henry, looking at it.

The captain of the *Golden Bounty* looked at his first mate. "I told you we needed a better marketing campaign," he said. "It's all about blueberries these days. Kids don't even know what a pineapple is anymore!"

"I know it's a pineapple," said Henry, looking at the pineapple. "Duh! I just mean— Is that all you've got down there?"

"There's no 'just' about it, young man," said the

captain. "Don't you know how much vitamin C a single pineapple contains? And we have twenty thousand of those bad boys on board!"

"But . . . don't you have any treasure? Aren't you pirates?" asked Uncle Clyde.

The captain laughed. "Good one!" he said. "No—we're in the fruit transport business."

Imogen felt a flash of satisfaction. Her guesses had been pretty close. But then she saw the disappointment on her family's faces, and the fury on Ava's, and the satisfaction faded.

And then she heard a scream. It seemed to be coming from the sky. . . . She looked up and saw something zooming through the air toward them. . . .

"Is it a bird?" said Nick.

"Is it a plane?" asked Nate.

"Is it a hallucination caused by eating too much brie at the buffet?" asked Josephine.

But it wasn't any of those things. It was a man, wearing a jet pack and a strange, lumpy gray costume that looked a bit like a shell. He swooped just above the Crims' heads and sprayed them all with high-powered squirt guns. And then he caught sight of Imogen, Ava, and Delia on the cruise ship, and he swooped down to attack them too.

"COMING IN HOT!" he shouted as he sprayed them with water.

"Is he a superhero?" Imogen whispered to Ava as they ducked behind a safety buoy.

Ava nodded. "More of a B-list one, though. *Such* a pathetic catchphrase. That water isn't even warm." She sighed. "This is the Mussel," she went on, over the shouts and screams of the Crims on the *Golden Bounty.* "He's the Gull's sidekick."

AVA, IMOGEN, AND Delia crouched below the side of the cruise ship while the strange, gray superhero continued his attack on the ship below.

"Is he, like, supposed to be . . . seafood?" asked Delia.

"Yep," said Ava. "It's a pretty ridiculous brand. But the potential for puns is phenomenal, so that should make your family happy at least."

"Congratulations for using the letter *P* so many times in that sentence," said Imogen.

"Thanks."

They ducked again as the Mussel jet packed in their direction and aimed another spray at them.

"Ugh," said Imogen, squeezing water out of her T-shirt. "It's salty!"

Down on the ship below, the Crims were chattering excitedly.

"Did you hear that?" asked Uncle Clyde. "We're so terrifying and dangerous that an actual superhero has come to battle us!"

"But that's marvelous!" cried Josephine. "Maybe we'll finally get to appear on *Britain's Got Talented Criminals*!"

Ava tutted. "That says everything you need to know about your family," she said. "They aren't ambitious enough. We should be insulted that the Gull sent only his loser of a sidekick after us. Can't he be bothered to attack us himself?"

"I didn't think we wanted him to attack us, though," said Imogen. "I thought we were supposed to be raiding his island without him noticing?"

"But he has noticed, or the Mussel wouldn't be here," said Ava. She peeped over the railing of the cruise ship to see what he was doing. "Look at him," she muttered. "What a loser."

But the Mussel didn't actually seem like a loser to Imogen. He had used his squirt gun to force the Crims—and the unfortunate crew of the *Golden Bounty*, who were just trying to transport their pineapples—into a group on the *Golden Bounty*'s deck. It was a bit like watching a sheepdog herd sheep. Except that instead of a dog, he was a flying human-shellfish hybrid who kept shouting things like "Mussel power!" And instead of sheep, they were a group of hardened criminals and confused fruit salespeople who kept shouting things like "Just WAIT till *Conman Weekly* magazine hears about this!" and "Remember when everyone used to serve cheese and pineapple on sticks at cocktail parties? Those were the good old days. . . ."

The Mussel pulled out a huge club-like weapon from deep within his shell and threatened the Crims with it. "No funny business," he said. "Or I'll scallop you!"

"What's scalloping?" Delia whispered to Imogen.

"Scalp, scallop," said Imogen. "It's another terrible pun."

"*Really* terrible," agreed Ava. "That thing is way too blunt to scalp people with, anyway. Want to see my scalping knife?" She pulled it out of her pocket and handed it over to Imogen and Delia to admire.

"Wow!" said Delia. "It's so cute and sharp!"

Then they heard another shout from the *Golden Bounty*, and they peered over the railing again.

"WOULD YOU MIND NOT WAVING THAT CLUB SO CLOSE TO MY FACE?" Uncle Knuckles was saying. "I'VE BEEN USING A FACE MASK EVERY NIGHT TO REDUCE THE NATURAL REDNESS OF MY SKIN TONE, AND BEING SMASHED IN THE FOREHEAD WOULD REALLY UNDO ALL MY HARD WORK."

"This isn't a club," said the Mussel, scowling (at least, he sounded as if he were scowling—his face wasn't really visible beneath the strange shell costume). "It's a foot."

"Mussels don't have feet," said Sam, still holding the (very unhappy-looking) ship's cat.

The Mussel (probably) rolled his eyes. "Shellfish anatomy is so misunderstood!" he said. "Every mussel has a foot—a muscular organ shaped like an ax that it uses to pull itself across sand."

Big Nana shook her head. "If a superhero has to explain his weapon, he's using the wrong weapon," she said. "You never have to explain a machine gun."

"SHUT UP!" shouted the Mussel, aiming the "foot" at the Crims, as if he wanted to knock them into the sea. "IT'S TIME TO TAKE OUT THE TRASH!"

Imogen frowned. "That's quite a weird thing for a mussel to say," she said.

Ava nodded. "The Gull and the Mussel need a refresher course at staying on brand."

"I think you could do with a better catchphrase," Sam said to the Mussel. "What about, 'It's time to show you my mussel?' Or 'If you're selfish, you'll have to answer to the shellfish.' Or 'I'll make you a shell of your former self'? Or 'Things are about to get salty!' Or—"

But the Mussel didn't seem to like any of Sam's ideas, because he swiped his foot at them again.

"Fair enough," said Sam, ducking just in time.

"What shall we do?" Imogen hissed to Ava as the Mussel swung the club toward the Crims again.

Ava shrugged. "I say we let the Mussel kill them all. They were stupid enough to attack the *Golden Bounty*. And stupid people deserve to die. Survival of the fittest, and all that."

"You really think the Mussel is the fittest?" said Imogen, and she had a point; the foot-club was obviously heavier than it looked, because the Mussel was now panting and slightly out of breath.

"Whatever," said Ava, shrugging again. "The point is, we don't need your family. Apart from Big Nana, obviously. We'll get her to tell us where the treasure is, and then we'll kill her too."

Imogen panicked. "We *do* need them . . . ," she said, hoping that she'd think of a convincing reason by the end of the sentence. And then she thought of something. *Thank you, brain. I promise to feed you lots of Brazil nuts and fish if I get out of this alive.* "Big Nana has a plan to stop you from killing us or maiming us or throwing any of us overboard," she continued. She stood up and looked down at Big Nana, who was squashed between Uncle Clyde and Delia on the deck of the *Golden Bounty*, like a very old, evil sandwich filling. "Isn't that right, Big Nana? Each member of the family knows one line of the directions to the buried treasure.

So if even one Crim dies, we won't know where to dig. . . ." She widened her eyes as she looked at her grandmother. *Please catch on. . . .*

Big Nana beamed up at Imogen like a bedside lamp that you've forgotten to turn off. "That's right, my salty piece of feta cheese!" she said.

Ava stood up and crossed her arms. "But if you've taught each member of the family one line of the directions to the treasure, then you must know all the directions yourself. So, like I said, you're the only one I need to keep alive."

"I'd anticipated that, you nasty boiled egg!" said Big Nana. "Which is why I hypnotized myself to forget all of them. Except the line I assigned myself, obviously."

Ava turned to look at Imogen, her eyes narrowed. "Is this true?"

"It's true," said Imogen.

"Extremely true," said Delia.

"I wasn't talking to you," snapped Ava. She sighed. "Fine," she said. "I guess I'll help you defeat the Mussel, then." She pulled out her anti-aircraft gun and fired it at the Mussel.

"Oh yeah," said Imogen. "I forgot there was a cannon on this ship." She ran over to it and started firing at the Mussel too.

The Mussel ducked and weaved as the Crims cheered

Ava and Imogen on, but then his jet pack started to sputter.

"He's running out of fuel!" said Imogen, reloading the cannon. "Let's get him!"

But the Mussel wasn't stupid enough to stay and fight. He jetted slowly off into the distance like a nasty case of food poisoning.

"He's gone!" cheered the Crims.

"Bravo!" The cruise ship passengers applauded, leaning out over their deck—they still thought the whole thing was a show for their entertainment. Cruise ship passengers can be very self-centered.

"That guy playing the Mussel was amazing!" said Kevin. "You couldn't even see the wires holding him up!"

Sam went down to the *Golden Bounty*'s hold and came back with an armful of pineapples. "Let's go to the cruise ship and celebrate with piña coladas!"

The Crims swarmed back from the *Golden Bounty* to the cruise ship—Uncle Knuckles gave Big Nana a hand, because her arthritis was acting up—and they headed straight for the bar on the pool deck.

"Hey!" shouted the captain of the *Golden Bounty*, stumbling onto the deck of the cruise ship. "Those pineapples are ours!" But then he stopped complaining and looked around. The cruise ship was a lot more luxurious than the *Golden Bounty*. He opened the door to one of the luxury cabins and saw the individual chocolates on the pillows and the Jacuzzis in the bathrooms. "I take it back," he said. "You can have the pineapples. As long as you don't mind me and my crew tagging along with you for a bit. . . . If our boss asks why we abandoned our boat and went on a three-week cruise to Aruba, you just tell her you kidnapped us. Okay?"

"No problem at all," said Uncle Clyde, who, as we know, enjoyed taking credit for crimes he hadn't committed.

Sam handed Uncle Knuckles the pineapples, and Uncle Knuckles smashed them with his bare fists to make pineapple juice. They mixed up fifty piña coladas and handed them out as the tourists and the pineapple sailors and the Crims all mingled together by the pool. The captain of the *Golden Bounty* played a game of blackjack with Freddie and ended up losing all his money, but he'd had a couple of piña coladas by that point, so he didn't really mind. After everyone had finished their drinks, Sam clapped his hands. "Please join me in the cabaret theater for my one-man performance of *Chicago*!" he said.

Everyone sang along and tapped their feet as Sam high-kicked and bowler-hatted his way through the entire musical, single-handedly. Sure, his voice was so low that no one could actually hear all the notes, but that wasn't necessarily a bad thing.

Imogen took a seat next to Delia in the back row.

"See?" she whispered to her cousin. "All's well that ends well."

Delia turned to her and scowled. "Don't quote Shakespeare at me, you overeducated traitor," she whispered. "And don't think I'm going to forgive you for choosing Ava over your family."

Imogen stared at her. "But we were getting along fine during the Mussel's attack!"

"Of course we were getting along fine!" said Delia. "Ava is a literal psychopath, and she was holding an anti-aircraft gun at the time! You know what Big Nana always says: 'When someone is pointing a large gun at you, it's best to be polite.'" She put on the whiny, high-pitched voice she used when she was making fun of Ava, and said, "'I say we let the Mussel kill them all.'"

Imogen's stomach grew cold. "You heard that?"

"Of course I heard," said Delia. "You know hearing tests are the only tests I ever pass." She shook her head. "You'll be sorry. Ava's not actually your friend." And she got up and walked away, leaving Imogen feeling scared and guilty and angry at the same time—her three least favorite emotions.

LIFE ON THE cruise ship carried on as normally as life on a cruise ship that's been hijacked by criminals and filled with pineapple shippers can be. Aunt Bets tried to disembowel Barbara with pineapple spikes, because Barbara told her she "liked her wig;" Isabella taught herself to drive the cruise ship by watching a couple of YouTube videos and took over as captain. (The real captain kept hearing people saying the word "and," which meant he kept thinking he was a chicken, which meant he was not very good at steering.) Isabella made a fantastic captain, although she did have to stand on a box full of pineapples to reach the steering wheel, and her announcements were mostly her blowing raspberries and singing "Twinkle, Twinkle, Little Star."

Imogen felt almost happy again. Everyone seemed to be getting along brilliantly—the crew of the *Golden Bounty* played water polo in the pool with the tourists, Uncle Clyde and Kevin started playing table tennis together every night after dinner, and Barbara began teaching a line dancing class in the cabaret theater every evening, which was very popular with Josephine and Uncle Knuckles. Several of the tourists had played so many games of poker that they now owed Freddie money, but Freddie was in a relaxed, happy vacation mood, and he decided not to use violence to collect their debts. Plus, Ava hadn't mentioned murdering any of Imogen's family members for at least three days. The only thing bothering her was the fact that Delia was still ignoring her.

But soon, Delia would become the least of Imogen's problems.

One afternoon, Imogen was in the Jacuzzi with Big Nana, who was very fond of bubbles, when she overheard Kevin muttering about how it was oddly warm for the North Sea. "I mean, it could be global warming," he said to Barbara, "but surely it shouldn't take two weeks to get to Oslo?"

"Wait," said the captain of the *Golden Bounty*. "You think we're going to *Norway*?"

Imogen's heart sank like the glass full of virgin piña colada she had just dropped in the Jacuzzi. She pulled herself out of the Jacuzzi and ran, swimsuit dripping, to the control room. She had to try something, anything, to distract the passengers. . . .

She grabbed the microphone and made an announcement. "Attention, passengers!" she said. "I'm pleased to say that we're starting happy hour three hours early today! And the first people at the bar get free chips!"

But she could still hear Kevin muttering to Barbara on the deck below: "The chips are free, anyway. Something fishy's going on. And not fishy in a good way, like a delicious fillet of salmon. . . ."

Barbara shaded her eyes against the sun and looked up at Imogen. "Hey! Yes, you, young lady!" she said. "I'm hearing rumors that we're not headed to Norway! If that's so, I insist that you turn this ship around at once!"

Imogen ran to the beauty lounge, where her mother was giving Ava a manicure.

"Darling!" said Josephine. "Have you come to get a pedicure? Very sensible. Your toes are looking disastrous at the moment. Like shriveled peas!"

"No," said Imogen, sitting down on the swivel chair next to Ava. "We have a major problem on our hands."

"*You* might," said Josephine, "but Ava has cuticle oil on *her* hands."

Imogen ignored her mother and turned to Ava. "The tourists have figured out that we're not going to Norway. They're beginning to revolt."

"They've always been revolting," said Ava, admiring her newly painted nails.

"That's a really old joke," said Imogen. "You can do better than that."

"I prefer to think of it as vintage," said Ava. "Anyway, isn't this something you can deal with on your own? Try distracting them or something. These are people who are voluntarily spending three weeks on a boat with an all-you-can-eat buffet. They're easily pleased. Throw them some peanuts, or something."

"I've tried that— They're not having any of it. They're shouting at us to turn around. You might not know how Uncle Knuckles gets when people shout, but—"

From somewhere on the boat, they could hear Uncle Knuckles wailing. "WHY CAN'T EVERYONE JUST LOVE ONE ANOTHER AND GET ALONG?"

Ava sighed and flicked her shiny ponytail. "Fine," she said. She took out her smartphone and loaded a map. "Oh, we're going to be fine," she said, studying it. "We're almost at Barbados. I have a plan. Don't worry."

Josephine laughed. "That's like telling Aunt Bets not

to murder innocent people with household objects! Or telling Al not to do so many crosswords! Or telling me not to be a style icon!"

Ava pushed back her chair and stood up, flicking her hands to dry her nails.

"Wait!" said Josephine, rushing over to her with another bottle of nail polish. "I haven't put the topcoat on! Big Nana always says: 'Always finish what you've started, especially murders and manicures.'"

"I'll be back in a minute," said Ava. "I just need to go and make an announcement to the passengers. . . ."

"Good morning, ladies, gentlemen, and Henry." Ava's voice crackled over the ship's loudspeaker. "I am pleased to tell you that we'll be docking in Norway in just a few hours. As you all know, it's extremely hot in Norway at this time of year, and this is palm tree season in northern Europe. The traditional Norwegian carnival will be starting in a few hours, so don't be surprised if you hear reggae music and see people drinking rum cocktails. . . ."

Imogen could see the crew of the *Golden Bounty* looking around, confused. She ushered them into the cabaret theater.

"Look," she said. "If you guys pretend to be really excited about going to Norway, we'll let you out in Barbados with the tourists. Otherwise, we'll let Henry conduct his fire experiments on you. Which will involve being burned to death by a really incompetent pyromaniac. The choice is yours."

The crew were on their very best behavior after that. Although the captain did eat all the bacon at the buffet at breakfast.

When the ship docked in Barbados, the cruise passengers and the crew of the *Golden Bounty* happily walked down the ramp off the ship, snapping photographs of the clear Caribbean waters and the flying fish and the stalls serving coconut bread.

The Crims waved them off happily. All except Uncle Knuckles, who waved them off sadly; he had grown rather fond of Barbara, who had taught him various herbal remedies to help him sleep, and Kevin, who had taught him the names of every species of Norwegian bird. "DON'T FORGET TO WRITE!" he shouted as the last tourist left the ship.

"Please don't tell me you've given them your address," said Ava as Uncle Knuckles cried massive tears into the sea, which raised the sea levels and caused a major flood in a nearby fishing village.

Uncle Knuckles cried even harder. "I FORGOT!" he cried.

"Thank badness for that," said Ava as the tourists started

looking around them and muttering about not being able to see glaciers or the northern lights and asking why people were speaking English. "Isabella, start the engines!"

As the cruise ship pulled away from the port, Ava wiped her hands (taking care not to smudge her nails) and said, "Right. That's taken care of."

The Crims all cheered—apart from Delia, who rolled her eyes, and Sam, who looked very sad, even though he was wearing a sequined cabaret outfit, and it's very hard to look sad in a sequined cabaret outfit.

"What's the matter with you?" asked Ava.

"Nothing," said Sam. "It's just— I'll miss them. I've never had fans before."

"You still have me," said Uncle Clyde, clapping Sam on the shoulder. "I'm really looking forward to your twelve o'clock show. Will you do that *Wicked* medley again?"

"We don't have time for bad off-off-off-Broadway performances," said Ava. "It's time to find Captain Glitterbeard's treasure."

"That's my favorite time!" said Uncle Clyde.

"Good," said Ava. "I hope you're all ready."

"We were *born* ready," said Big Nana, who occasionally said things that made her sound like an eccentric motivational speaker. "This treasure is our birthright!"

Imogen felt a flash of guilt—she was about to give most

of her family's birthright to Ava. But then she remembered that Big Nana was born a Kruk before fleeing the family in her twenties . . . so wasn't the treasure Ava's birthright too, sort of?

(That's the good thing about being as clever as Imogen. You can justify anything to yourself.)

The cruise ship did seem very big and empty without the tourists. The Crims felt deflated without their new friends, like lonely car tires. Since they hadn't arrived at the island yet, Sam performed his twelve o'clock show as usual, but Uncle Knuckles was the only one who went to see it, and he tried to sing along, which was very upsetting for everyone on the ship. Uncle Knuckles tried playing table tennis on his own, but there was no one to return his shots, so all the balls sailed into the sea. Big Nana had a Jacuzzi to herself. (She was quite happy about that, actually.)

Isabella was steering the ship to the island off the coast of Jamaica, where Captain Glitterbeard's treasure was hidden. According to Big Nana, they just had a few miles to go. And the closer they got to the island, the more nervous Imogen became. How was she going to save her family if the treasure didn't exist? How was she going to save them if it *did* exist? Imogen wished there was someone she could talk through her dilemma with. She wished she could confide in Delia. She looked over at her cousin, lying on a lounger, music blaring out of her headphones, wearing a black T-shirt with a slogan on it that said "I Hate You. Yes You, Imogen Crim." She suddenly wished she was back in Delia's bedroom, eating pizza and planning a nice simple crime, like a mugging or a school bus hijacking.

A few hours later, the Crims' ship drifted up to the white-sand beach of Captain Glitterbeard's island. Imogen closed her eyes and breathed in the fresh air. Birds were tweeting relaxingly. Waves were lapping at the shore soothingly. Palm trees were swaying in the wind calmingly. And Big Nana was shouting at all the Crims. "Hurry up and steal black clothes from the tourists' cabins now, you burned roast potatoes, before I garrote you with my dental floss." Which wasn't very relaxing at all.

"Why do we need to wear black?" asked Sam.

"Because it's the coolest color," said Henry, who only ever wore black, anyway; he thought it reflected the darkness and depth of his soul.

"We have to wear black because that's what cat burglars wear," said Big Nana.

"Why would we want to burgle a cat?" said Nick.

"Yeah," said Nate. "Cats don't have anything to steal. Except cat food. And that really doesn't taste good, unless you eat it with a lot of mustard."

Big Nana closed her eyes and took a deep breath. "We aren't going to burgle a cat, you twin pack of store-brand cereal bars. We just don't want anyone to notice us while we're hunting for Captain Glitterbeard's treasure. Now, weigh the anchor and lower the lifeboat into the water, so we can get closer to the shore."

Nick and Nate lowered the lifeboat into the water, and everyone climbed in, one by one, until the little ship was positively infested with Crims. Ava was the last to climb in. She sat on Imogen's head. "What?" she said when Imogen tried to shove her off. "This is the cleanest place on the boat."

Imogen decided to take it as a compliment. She had just shampooed her hair that morning. It was nice that someone had noticed.

"To the island!" cried Big Nana, and Nick and Nate took an oar each and began to row to shore.

"There's a hole in the bottom of this lifeboat," said Nick, looking down. Water was flooding in and was up to their ankles.

"Then you'll just have to row quickly, won't you?" said Big Nana.

The Crims sang pirate shanties as the twins rowed the little boat through the water. But by the time they reached the beach, they were practically swimming.

"We made it!" said Nate, as the Crims tumbled out

onto the beach. But then he looked out at something in the distance . . . "Wait," he said. "Where's the cruise ship gone?"

Imogen turned to look. Sure enough, the cruise ship was not where they'd left it. And then she spotted a teeny, tiny ship just disappearing over the horizon.

"You revolting ready meals!" screamed Big Nana. "Didn't any of you weigh the anchor like I asked?"

"Isabella was the captain," said Uncle Clyde. "That was her job."

"Captain," babbled Isabella, pointing to herself.

"She's practically a baby!" shouted Big Nana.

"Then the *actual* captain should have done it," said Nick.

But the actual captain was still on the cruise ship, drifting off into the distance, dreaming about laying some eggs.

"Don't tell me we're going to be stuck here forever," Imogen said.

"Okay," said Sam. "But that won't make it any less true."

Ava let out a roar—the sort of roar someone would let out if they were descended from dinosaurs but didn't know it yet. (In fact, the Kruks were distantly related to the *Tyrannosaurus rex*, which is why they all had such powerful bites and tiny hands.) "You morons!" she shouted. She wasn't as good at coming up with insults as Big Nana, but then she was young, so there was still time to grow. "How are we going to get out of here now?"

"Well," said Imogen, "once we have the treasure, we'll be able to rent a ship. Or buy one. Or pay a ship designer to make one especially for us, complete with a karaoke machine. Depending on how big this treasure haul turns out to be . . ."

"I think we could do without the karaoke machine," said Ava. "But okay. I get your point."

Big Nana clapped her hands to get everyone's attention. "Seeing as we have lost our only way of escaping the island," she said, "it's more important than ever that we find Captain Glitterbeard's treasure. There's a shipwreck on the other side of this island. We have to walk through a rain forest to get there. And when we get there, I'll give you all the first line of directions to find the treasure. Can the rest of you remember the lines you've memorized?"

"Yes," chanted the Crims.

Imogen was relieved. If Captain Glitterbeard's treasure didn't exist, Big Nana wouldn't be so keen on finding it. And she'd be a lot more concerned about getting off the island. And would she really have gone to all the effort of pulling the Crims aside, one by one, and making them remember a line of directions to treasure that didn't even exist? She grinned at Ava as they started to push aside the undergrowth and pick their way through the rain forest.

Ava grinned back. *See?* thought Imogen. *Ava's not a psychopath, really.*

The island was bigger than it looked, and the rain forest was harder to walk through than Imogen had expected. She was wearing sandals and shorts, so her legs kept getting scratched by twigs and bitten by mosquitos.

"I'm tired," moaned Henry.

"I'm tired of you," said Big Nana. "So be quiet, or I'll feed you to that puma."

The Crims all jumped, very quietly, so as not to attract the puma's attention.

"This better be worth it," said Delia, treading on Imogen's toe. Probably on purpose.

The rain forest was as beautiful as it was deadly. Imogen looked up at the clear blue sky through the canopy of trees. Huge butterflies were flitting across the sky, and there was an unusual-looking tropical bird sitting in the palm tree just above her head.

"Duck," whispered Ava.

"I think it's an ibis, actually," said Imogen, standing on tiptoe to get a closer look.

"No, loser," hissed Ava. "Duck!" She grabbed Imogen by the arm and pulled her down into the undergrowth—and seconds later, a machine gun appeared from between the leaves of a nearby palm tree and sent a volley of bullets toward them across the rain forest.

"Ah yes," said Big Nana as the Crims all dropped to the floor. "I forgot to mention—there's quite a lot of security on this island. No one knows who owns it, but he's revoltingly rich and extremely paranoid and very deadly."

"Nuts!" said Uncle Clyde.

"Well, quite, my little flame-retardant sponge cake," said Big Nana, poking her head above the undergrowth to see whether the coast was clear.

"No!" said Uncle Clyde, pointing to the coconuts that were tumbling out of the sky toward them. "Nuts!" They were the shiniest coconuts Imogen had ever seen. And as they got closer, she realized why: They were embedded with silver razor blades.

"You didn't think you ought to mention the crazy paranoid billionaire before you took us to the island?" said Ava as the Crims ran for safety.

"A little knowledge is a dangerous thing," said Big Nana, panting. "Almost as dangerous as a little robotic monkey, armed with a grenade . . ."

Imogen froze. Because there was a little robotic monkey, armed with a grenade, right in front of her, and it was raising its arm to throw it in her direction—but before it could, Isabella leaped up and wrestled the monkey to the ground. She snatched the grenade from its fingers and swallowed it whole. Which sounds like a terrible idea, but wasn't, because she suffered from a gunpowder deficiency.

"Like I said," said Ava, giving Isabella a little high five, "you could have warned us."

"But we're all supervillains here, aren't we?" said Big Nana, stepping over a land mine and carrying on through the rain forest. "We love a bit of danger, don't we?"

Ava snorted. At the idea of the Crims being supervillains, Imogen guessed, and not at the bit about loving danger.

"We'll just have to be on high alert," continued Big Nana, using her pirate sword to swipe the vegetation out of her way. "And if we get captured by security, we'll just tell them that Sam is a cabaret singer who has come to the island to perform a gig, and we're all his entourage."

Sam nodded sadly. He still missed his fans.

"Anyway," said Big Nana, "I really need a wee. And like I always say, 'You should never wee in the middle of a rain forest unless you're an iguana or an elderly explorer with bladder problems.' I'll meet you at the shipwreck."

Imogen opened her mouth to argue, but Big Nana had already disappeared into the undergrowth like a large red-haired badger. Why did her grandmother always abandon them at times of crisis?

Imogen, Ava, and the rest of the Crims carried on through the rain forest, edging their way past killer sloths and mutant crocodiles and babbling brooks made of hydrochloric acid. At last, the trees cleared, and they saw the skeletal remains of the shipwreck silhouetted against the sky on the beach in front of them.

"We've made it!" said Uncle Clyde, breaking into a run.

But they hadn't made it.

Because that's when a group of guards, dressed in camouflage and carrying very nasty-looking guns, appeared from out of the forest and surrounded them.

"What are you doing here?" said the biggest and scariest guard, pointing his gun at Imogen.

Think, Imogen told herself. But she couldn't think. She was too busy sweating and being terrified.

The less scary guards raised their guns too.

Guns. That's it! thought Imogen. *Ava has about thirty of those things in her surprisingly spacious pockets!*

She shot Ava a look, as if to say "What happened to your portable cannon?"

And Ava shot one back, as if to say "I must have left it behind on the cruise ship."

But just then, Big Nana popped up from the undergrowth and said, "Ooh! Great! An armed escort!"

The guards turned their guns on Big Nana.

"What did the muddy old woman say?" said the biggest, scariest guard to the smallest, least scary guard. Because Big Nana was, for some reason, covered in mud.

Big Nana pointed at Sam. "Aren't you here to escort

the Magnificent Sam to the owner of this island? He's due to perform his legendary *Wicked* medley in half an hour's time!"

The guards looked at one another. "He didn't mention anyone coming to perform," said the biggest, scariest guard.

"But he didn't mention anyone *not* coming to perform," said the smallest, least scary guard.

"And he really does love amateur musicians singing Broadway medleys, for some reason," said an average-sized, mildly assertive guard.

The biggest, scariest guard shrugged. "All right, then," he said. "I suppose you'd better come with us. . . ."

Imogen felt sick. She really didn't want to know who "he" was. But she was about to find out.

The guards marched them past the shipwreck and along the beach to another patch of rain forest. They stopped in front of some thick, twisting vines. Imogen was confused— Was this mysterious man hiding out back on the other side of the rain forest? Were they going to have to deal with that monkey again? But then she saw it: a huge set of iron gates, hidden behind vines. Whoever it was lived right here.

To get into the compound, the Crims had to pass through fingerprint security, retinal scanners, and an army assault course. Then they walked across a beautifully manicured lawn until they reached a huge, imposing mansion, painted a revolting shade of pink, with fake columns and fake chimneys and roof tiles made of fake money. At least, Imogen assumed it was fake money. . . .

"Whoever lives here is obviously really powerful," whispered Josephine, reapplying her lipstick as the guards led them up the stone steps into the mansion itself.

"And he obviously has terrible taste in architecture," muttered Imogen as they walked through the marble hallways, which were lined, for some reason, with action film posters.

"Whoever he is, he's right there," whispered Ava as the guards led them into a large, velvet-padded room dominated by a huge, throne-like chair.

And then the Crims stopped speaking, and stood, huddled together in silence.

Because slowly, the chair had started to swivel round. . . .

THE CHAIR SPUN around . . . and sitting in it was a square-jawed, graying man with a very familiar-looking dent in his chin.

"Hey, guys," he said. His eyes narrowed when he smiled.

Imogen knew that smile. . . .

"It's Don Vadrolga!"

The Crims were all very excited. Don Vadrolga was the star of many of their favorite movies, including *Barry*, a horror film about a psychic girl with a boy's name, and *Sunday Morning Temperature*, a cult hit from the 1970s. Don was famous for being cool, for being an amazing dancer, and for having a slightly revolting ponytail. But the ponytail was gone. Imogen thought he looked pretty good, for an extremely famous person who has, until quite recently, been held hostage by an extremely famous crime family for an extremely long time.

"I know you danced with a princess once," said Josephine, rubbing his arm. "I wonder— Would you maybe dance with me later? Some say she and I have lots in common. Our clothes, mostly, because I stole all my formal gowns from her wardrobe."

"I THOUGHT YOU WERE WONDERFUL IN THAT FILM WHERE YOU'RE A SPY AND YOU HAVE TO BE LOWERED FROM THE CEILING SO THAT THE SENSORS ON THE FLOOR DON'T SPOT YOU," said Uncle Knuckles.

"That wasn't me," said Don Vadrolga. "That was Tom Cruise."

"Well, I loved you in *Jerry Maguire*," said Freddie.

"Again, a Tom Cruise film," said Don Vadrolga.

"You were fantastic in that movie with the talking baby!" said Uncle Clyde.

"Thank you," said Don Vadrolga, smiling his crinkly smile. "A film I actually appeared in."

"It was so cute the way you commented on everything that was going on, even though you were just a baby!"

Don Vadrolga stopped smiling. "That wasn't me. I

played the hero! The love interest! Are you seriously confusing me with a newborn baby who didn't even grow up to be a famous actor? What's *wrong* with you?"

"I don't know," said Ava, stepping forward, eyes furious. "What's wrong with YOU?"

As soon as Don saw Ava, he stood up and started shaking. And not because he was doing a very familiar disco dance move. "No!" he cried, clutching his chair, as if it could help him, which it couldn't. "Not her! She can't bring me back there!"

"WHAT ARE YOU DOING HERE?" Ava shouted.

But Don Vadrolga didn't reply. Instead, he leaped out of his chair and ran out of the room. And he actually looked pretty cool doing it, too, because he was Don Vadrolga.

The Crims and Ava ran after Don Vadrolga, through the mansion, out of the back door, over the manicured lawn, past the hedges that had been topiaried to look like characters from Don Vadrolga movies, and back through the booby-trapped jungle. Panting and breathless, they somehow made it all the way to a clearing in the middle of the rain forest that they hadn't come across before. A private plane was waiting on the grassy runway. But it didn't wait very long, because Don Vadrolga was already running up the steps into the plane.

"The traitor!" Ava screamed, still running toward the

plane, as Don Vadrolga started the engine. She staggered to a stop as the plane soared into the air. "The only reason he knows how to fly a plane is because Luka gave him flying lessons. He used to fly my brothers and sisters to their Italian classes in Rome, and their flamenco classes in Seville, and their capitalism classes in New York. And how did he thank us? He abandoned the family when we needed him most! He wasn't there to release the tigers when the Gull attacked Krukingham Palace, so Uncle Dedrick and cousin Violet got arrested! And Luka has probably been arrested too by now, because Violet is such a little snitch. I miss her so much." Ava tried to cry, but she couldn't, because she was a Kruk.

Big Nana put an arm around Ava's shoulders, and then she took it off again, because it looked as though Ava was about to hit her. "Well, my buttered crumpet," said Big Nana, "at least it will be easier for us to find the treasure without Don Vadrolga around."

Ava nodded. But her fists were still clenched.

Imogen was nervous. *Please let the treasure be worth something. . . .* She knew what Ava was like when she was disappointed: psychopathic, violent, fond of hurting people with saws . . .

"Right," said Big Nana. "Enough of being distracted by faded Hollywood stars. It's time for me to give you the first set of directions to the treasure."

The Crims cheered half-heartedly—to be honest, they'd had quite enough of nearly dying for one day. But Uncle Clyde still seemed very excited about the whole thing. He loved treasure hunts almost as much as he loved coming up with ridiculous ideas for crimes that would almost certainly fail. "Tell me! Tell me!" he said, jumping up and down in front of Big Nana like a terrible pogo stick.

"Right," said Big Nana. "Here's the clue: *Walk through the thickest brambles you've ever seen. Stop when something makes you scream.*"

"This way!" shouted Uncle Clyde, running headfirst into a thicket of thorns. The rest of the Crims tramped after him, shouting out their favorite swear words whenever the thorns scraped their ankles and shins and faces. And then they stopped, because Uncle Clyde was staring at a tree trunk and screaming.

"The pattern in the bark!" he shrieked, pointing at the tree. "If you squint, it looks a bit like Mother Teresa!"

The Crims were no fans of Mother Teresa—she had taken a vow of poverty and dedicated her life to helping others. She had even been made a saint. In other words, she was the opposite of everything the Crims stood for.

"Excellent, Clyde, you inedible wallaby," said Big Nana. "Let's hear your clue next."

Uncle Clyde rubbed his hands and recited the next set

of directions: *"Find a group of vicious jaguars and follow them, like a guiding star."*

"That doesn't sound remotely dangerous or terrifying," said Imogen as they walked through the rain forest, searching for animals that any sane person would stay far away from. She often resorted to sarcasm in difficult situations.

They were tiptoeing around the edge of a crocodile-infested swamp when Henry, who was leading the group, stopped. "There," he whispered.

"Jaguars?" whispered Delia.

"No," said Henry, looking around. "I was just thinking those bushes look really flammable. Nice dry twigs."

The Crims all groaned and then kept walking—but they didn't get far, because then Imogen actually spotted a pair of jaguars, slinking between the trees. She stared at them, awestruck by their beauty for a moment, before pointing them out to her family.

"Darling, well done," whispered Josephine. "I've been desperate for a new leopard-print coat. But jaguar will be even better!"

Jaguars, it turns out, don't really like being followed. They get a little growly, a little scratchy, and quite a bit bite-y. Luckily, as soon as the jaguars turned on them, the Crims all ran away as fast as they could, and the only person the jaguars managed to attack was Uncle Knuckles. His limbs were so tough that the jaguars lost several teeth and then backed away from him apologetically.

"I'm beginning to wonder," panted Delia, once they were out of danger, "whether Captain Glitterbeard's treasure is worth all this effort."

"But it must be," said Sam, "if he went to this much trouble to hide it." Imogen noticed that Sam was shaking like a terrified leaf. He loved animals, but only if they were smaller than him.

"I suppose we're where the jaguars were supposed to lead us?" asked Imogen. But really, she wasn't sure. The directions seemed frustratingly nonspecific.

Still, Big Nana nodded and looked to Sam, who recited his directions next. They led them across a rocky ravine. Then Isabella recited hers, which were quite hard to understand, because she still couldn't say her *R*s properly. Al's clue led them through a swarm of mosquitos, and Josephine's took them up a sheer cliff face, and Nick's led them across a small but extremely hot desert—the private island featured a weirdly large number of microclimates.

"Please say we're nearly there," huffed Delia as they trekked up sand dunes and dodged spitting camels.

"We are, my uncomfortable suspenders," said Big Nana, pointing to the ground in front of her. "Look."

There, on the sand, was an *X* made of rocks.

"That's it?" asked Sam. "That's the treasure?"

"No," said Big Nana, sighing heavily (she had gained weight on the cruise because she had been determined to "get someone else's money's worth" from the buffet). "This is where we have to dig."

"Brilliant!" said Uncle Clyde. "Has anyone got a shovel?"

"Spade!" said Isabella, holding out the plastic toy shovel Imogen had bought her in Dullport.

"Anybody got a proper one?" asked Uncle Clyde.

There was an unwelcome silence. Which is saying something, because usually, when the Crims were involved, silence was like an oasis in a very shout-y desert.

Imogen was at the end of her rope with her family. And her rope hadn't been very long in the first place. "Seriously?" she said. "We come on a treasure hunt, and no one has brought a proper shovel?"

Delia looked at her. "Have *you* brought a shovel?" she asked.

"No," Imogen admitted, looking down at her feet, because they were never annoyed with her.

"Well, then," said Delia, who held out her hand. "Isabella, give that shovel to me."

Delia took a deep breath, took the shovel from Isabella,

and started digging. At least, she *tried* to start digging. It wasn't easy, because the ground was rock hard. Which wasn't surprising, as it was made of rocks.

Ava sat down on a patch of grass—*Just like her to find the only comfortable place to sit,* thought Imogen—and watched as, one by one, the Crims took turns with the toy shovel. No one lasted very long. Freddie was hopeless, because he spent too long calculating the best possible angle to dig at and no time actually digging. Henry set fire to the shovel and melted it, so everyone thought that was that, but then Isabella started gnawing her way through the rocks with her teeth, which was much more effective than the shovel had been. But even she took more than an hour to make a small dent in the ground.

"This dirt is like concrete," murmured Imogen.

"I think it *is* concrete," Freddie replied, scratching his fingernail over a piece of rubble that Isabella had chewed free. "How strange . . ."

"Don't be silly," Big Nana put in. "It's just a bunch of tiny rocks, stuck together. It happens all the time in Caribbean climates."

"I wish you'd told us that before we started digging," Delia moaned.

Miserable, aching, and humiliated, Imogen turned to Ava, who had produced a sun umbrella, deck chair, and fruity cocktail from her pockets and was lounging on her patch of grass, sipping her drink and reading *Chicken Soup for the Supercriminal's Soul.* "Aren't you going to help?" she asked.

"I thought you'd never ask!" said Ava. She reached into the back pocket of her jeans and pulled out a tiny but powerful pneumatic drill.

"That's cheating," said Aunt Bets, who didn't really believe in technology—the other Crims were always getting telegrams from her saying things like "I'll be home for dinner in an hour, once I've caught and killed a couple of pigs and turned them into bacon."

"Who cares if it's cheating?" said Josephine. "I'm sweating, and I haven't sweated since 1984, when I tried to steal a baton at the Olympics and ended up accidentally taking part in the 400-meter relay race."

So, Ava shrugged, walked over to where the *X* had been, and switched on her pneumatic drill. Imogen had an unnerving flashback to the last time she'd been around Ava and a power tool, when Ava had almost sawed her body in half and then blown her up for good measure (knowing when to stop wasn't Ava's strong point). But Ava did know when to stop this time—just a few seconds after she had started drilling, she turned off the drill and reached down into the hole she had made. She had hit something.

Ava pulled an object out of the sand. Everyone crowded round to see what it was.

"A treasure chest," whispered Delia, with the sort of

awe she usually reserved for the Instagram reveal of celebrity sportswear lines.

Imogen was relieved to see that it was, indeed, a treasure chest. (Her cousins weren't very good at describing things. Henry had once told her he'd stolen her a golden bracelet, and it turned out to be a rubber hand.) Ava brushed the sand off the treasure chest and held it out to Imogen. "You should open it," she said. "Captain Glitterbeard's your ancestor."

Imogen took the treasure chest from Ava and smiled. *Wow,* she thought. *Ava is much more generous than I'd given her credit for. Maybe she won't try to steal the treasure and kill us after all.*

And then Ava said, "Besides, it might be booby-trapped, and I like having all my fingers." Which was much more of an Ava thing to say.

Imogen took the box. *This is it. The moment of truth.*

She took a deep breath.

She let out the breath.

She took another deep breath.

"Get on with it!" yelled Uncle Clyde.

"LEAVE HER ALONE! SHE'S DOING MINDFUL BREATHING EXERCISES!" shouted Uncle Knuckles.

But Henry was trying to grab the chest off her now, so she pried it open. The hinges squeaked as the lid swung up. It opened more easily than she thought it would.

Imogen looked down.

But there wasn't gold inside the treasure chest.

There weren't jewels or precious stones of any kind.

There weren't long-lost paintings by Leonardo da Vinci, or original Shakespeare manuscripts or ancient Chinese pottery.

The only thing inside the box was a mirror.

It wasn't gold-plated. It wasn't inlaid with diamonds. It wasn't particularly big or particularly old. It didn't look as though it had once belonged to a Hollywood star or an evil Disney stepmother. The frame was plastic and the words "HENRY CRIM LOOKED AT HIMSELF IN THIS MIRROR" were etched on the outside. And the mirror itself was cracked. In other words, it wasn't worth very much at all.

"This isn't treasure," Imogen said. "This is seven years' bad luck." She looked at her grandmother, and everything started to make sense. Big Nana's sudden need to pee and the mud on her face . . . the "concrete" poured over the treasure . . .

"Where's the *actual* treasure?" Imogen asked. "Because you clearly brought this with you from home and buried it here when we weren't looking."

"*You're* the real treasure!" said Big Nana. "Look into

the mirror! It's all the Crims, working together to overcome a difficult obstacle!" She looked around at her family, with eyes full of love.

They looked back at her, with eyes full of hate.

"What?" said Imogen, horrified.

"What?" said Uncle Clyde, confused.

"Watt?" said Henry, who was trying to remember how electricity was measured. He was staring at Ava, who was vibrating as though an electric current was running through her. Imogen had a horrible feeling she was actually shaking with anger.

"You made up the *whole thing*?" asked Imogen. "About Captain Glitterbeard and the treasure? There isn't a hidden fortune buried somewhere on this island?"

This is okay, she told herself. *Take deep breaths. This isn't the worst thing that's ever happened to you. That was when Big Nana pretended to be dead and you cried yourself to sleep for two years. Or when Big Nana wrote that poison-pen letter and got you kicked out of the school you loved so much. Or when Big Nana lied to you and pretended she was a babysitter called Mrs. Teakettle for months. . . .* Now, she came to think of it, all her worst memories involved Big Nana. She shook her head. How could she have been so stupid? She should never have let herself trust her grandmother again.

"I didn't make it *all* up," said Big Nana. "We *are* related to Captain Glitterbeard. Only he was a pretty rubbish pirate. Actually, he was a pirate for only a few months before he settled in Nantucket and started a clambake business. So, I suppose I did lie, a little bit."

"But *why* did you lie?" Imogen asked.

Big Nana sighed. "I thought we could do with a bonding exercise, and the ropes course that everyone likes was booked up for months. But then you were all so awful in the caravan that I decided you didn't *deserve* a bonding course. Then we were on the cruise ship, and the Mussel was about to kill us, and I needed to think of something that would convince Ava to help save our lives . . . and Imogen brought up Captain Glitterbeard, and—" Big Nana stopped. "What's that growling noise?" she asked.

Everyone looked around to see where the sound was coming from.

"It sounds like a really lethal, high-pitched grizzly bear," said Sam.

"OR A MAMMOTH WITH INDIGESTION," said Uncle Knuckles. "EXCEPT THEY'RE EXTINCT, SO IT PROBABLY ISN'T THAT."

"Come on, children," said Big Nana. "What have I always taught you? 'If you can't identify an animal by its growl, you'll end up in its bowels.'"

Imogen looked across at Ava, whose fists were clenched,

and whose face was purple with rage, and whose teeth were bared (and, Imogen noticed, horribly pointy). . . .

"I think the noise is coming from Ava," Imogen said. "I think she still might be about to kill us."

And as Imogen spoke, Ava let out a terrifying roar.

"Excellent impression of a lion!" said Sam. "Can you teach me? Once you've finished murdering my grandmother?"

Because Ava was now standing over Big Nana, throttling her with her bare hands.

"HELP ME!" SHOUTED Big Nana, trying and failing to push Ava off her.

But Imogen was too angry to help. She just stood there and watched, her mind mostly blank, apart from the bit that was filled with anger at her grandmother.

The other Crims just stood there watching too. They didn't seem to know how to help, which was understandable—most children are taught to help others, and share, and cooperate, but the Crims were taught to steal from hospital patients and never say "please" and "thank you" except in an ironic way.

"Ava's strangling me!" shouted Big Nana, between gasps of breath.

"Duh," said Henry. "We can see that."

"And if you think about it, that's sort of a good thing," said Freddie. "Because she could be shooting at you with an anti-aircraft gun."

"Bets!" shouted Big Nana. "Come on! You're always going on about how you want to kill Ava! Now's your chance!"

Aunt Bets rustled around in her bag for her sharpened knitting needles, or her sharpened colostomy bag, or her sharpened packet of custard creams (she could sharpen anything), but she couldn't find any of them. She shrugged apologetically. "All I've got in here is an empty packet of acetaminophen, some receipts, and a tub of Vaseline," she said. "Ooh, and my cyanide-flavored cough drops! Ava, dear, would you like one?"

"No thanks," said Ava, carrying on with the throttling.

"Someone, please!" croaked Big Nana. "Help! Any-one!"

"Don't worry!" cried Uncle Clyde, his red hair waving as though it were trying to get everyone's attention, which it probably was (his hair had always wanted to be famous). "I have an idea! It's a little bit complicated. . . ."

Big Nana let out a sound that probably would have

been a groan if she'd been able to breathe properly.

Uncle Clyde got down on his hands and knees and searched the sand until he'd found what he'd been looking for: a scorpion. "Aha!" he cried, picking it up between his thumb and forefinger. "Just a moment, Mother!" He crept over to Ava, who was too busy leaning on Big Nana's windpipe to notice. He leaned in and tried to get the scorpion to sting her. The scorpion reared its tail . . . and then it stung Uncle Clyde instead. Which was only fair, really, seeing as he'd been the one to disturb its Tuesday afternoon. Uncle Clyde ended up writhing around in the sand, going into anaphylactic shock, until Imogen (always prepared) gave him an adrenaline shot.

"Clyde, you idiot!" Big Nana managed to choke out. "You're about as much use as sunscreen in the Antarctic!"

"Actually," said Ava, taking a break from throttling Big Nana because she loved correcting people almost as much as she loved killing people, "the sun can be quite strong in the Antarctic. Just because it's cold, that doesn't mean you don't need to protect yourself from harmful UV rays." And she started strangling Big Nana again.

"Imogen," croaked Big Nana, turning her sad blue eyes on her. "You're my only hope. . . ."

But Imogen was still shaking with fury. Once again, Big Nana had lied to her, and let her down, and made her feel like a fool (and not in a fun way like when she'd played the jester in the Crim family production of *Twelfth Night*). She looked down at her WWASVD bracelet. *A supervillain is loyal to no one,* she thought. *A supervillain would walk away and let Ava kill her entire family. That way, I'd inherit the family fortune: a dangerous house, a lot of stolen silverware, and Uncle Clyde's collection of 1990s boy band CDs.*

Big Nana reached out an arm to Imogen. She was shaking. "Please?" she croaked. Imogen remembered how devastated she had been when she'd heard about Big Nana's death in the Underwater Submarine Heist. And how empty life had seemed without her. Easier, yes. But so boring. Without Big Nana, Imogen had felt like a planet without a sun—just a pointless piece of rock. She looked down into Big Nana's eyes. She had never seen her grandmother look so weak. She was scared, Imogen realized. *Am I really just going to stand by and watch a shiny-haired murderer kill the most important person in my life?* she asked herself. There was no point denying it. She was a supervillain—or at least she wanted to be. But above everything else, she was a Crim.

She had to save Big Nana.

She ran over to Ava and grabbed her arms, pulling with all her strength to drag her off Big Nana. "Please don't let me be too late . . . ," she muttered. But Ava was too strong for her.

"Ugh, Imogen," she said. "What are you doing? You should be trying to help me! Do you know how much time this stupid fake treasure hunt has cost us? And do you know that you can't buy time? Because I tried once and it turned out to be a scam—"

"Excellent idea for a scam!" said Uncle Clyde.

"And you know that even supervillains don't live forever?" Ava continued. "Except the ones in New Mexico who have discovered the secret to eternal youth? And yes, I'm heading down to Albuquerque as soon as I've finished with the Gull. And yes, you can come with me. As long as you help me kill your grandmother first."

But Imogen kept trying to wrestle Ava away from Big Nana. "Uncle Knuckles!" she shouted. "Can you give me a hand?"

"I'D RATHER NOT, IF THAT'S OKAY," said Uncle Knuckles. "IT'S VERY CONVENIENT HAVING THEM BOTH ATTACHED TO THE ENDS OF MY ARMS. AND I'M NOT SURE I HAVE THE PERSONALITY TO PULL OFF A HOOK."

"No," said Imogen. "I mean, can you help me pull Ava off Big Nana?"

"WHY DIDN'T YOU SAY SO?" said Uncle Knuckles. He ran over and pulled at Ava's other arm, and soon, they all fell backward in a pile on the sand.

"Thank you," croaked Big Nana, rubbing her throat.

She staggered over to Ava's deck chair and took a sip of her fruity cocktail.

Ava turned to Imogen, eyes flashing like angry headlights, and said, "You really *are* a loser!" Then she turned and began to walk back the way they had come, toward the beach. Imogen followed Ava. The Crims followed Imogen. "I was a fool to think I could trust you! I was an idiot to think you would help me! I was an imbecile to think you were even close to my level. I was a— What's another word for 'fool'?"

"Buffoon?" suggested Al, shaking a poison frog from his shoulder.

Ava looked at him. "Is that a real word?"

"I think so. I am very fond of thesauruses."

"Fine," said Ava, looking over her shoulder to glare at Imogen. "I was a buffoon to ever think you'd put your crime-committing destiny above your pathetic family! They're like a noose around your neck! They ruin everything! Even Adele songs!"

"Hey," said Sam, put out. "You said you *loved* my cover of 'Someone Like You.'"

"I was LYING!" shouted Ava. "We're CRIMINALS, for badness' sake! Every other sentence is a lie!"

Imogen didn't want to fall out with Ava. She liked having a friend who was on her level. She just didn't want her to kill everyone that she loved. "Come on, Ava," she said. She moved to touch Ava's arm, but Ava pulled away. "What about our . . . Big Plan? This was just a side adventure, anyway, right?"

Ava laughed a nasty, cold laugh, like a cheap ice cream. "*We* don't have a Big Plan," she said. "*I* have a big plan. I've learned my lesson now. I don't need anyone. Not even a criminal with lovely hair and an excellent GPA. I am truly, totally, one hundred percent better off on my own."

Imogen felt a flash of fear. She could see where this was going, and she didn't like the look of the destination. "No," she said. "Come on, Ava . . ."

"Yes," said Ava. "I'm not just going to maroon your stupid family on this island—as you so helpfully suggested—I'm going to maroon you here too."

Imogen laughed nervously. She could feel her family glaring at her. (Except for Sam, who had taken a bite out of a mango filled with broken glass and was now picking out the shards.) "I suggested a *temporary* marooning," she said, looking around at them all. "I was always planning to come back and rescue you. . . ." But the others didn't look impressed. (Except for Sam, who was quite impressed at just how much glass could fit in a single mango.) In fact, they looked depressed. Which was fair enough, as one of their closest family members had been planning to abandon them on a desert island.

But then Imogen stopped worrying about what the

Crims thought of her and started worrying about Ava again. Because now that they had reached the beach once more, Ava had pulled her miniature cannon out of her pocket and was aiming it at the Crims as she walked toward the lifeboat. "Good riddance, losers!" she said. "Now, if you'll excuse me, I have a superhero's lair to infiltrate."

"Ava," said Freddie. "I hate to be helpful, but you know there's a massive hole in the bottom of that lifeboat?"

"Then it's lucky I have a boat puncture repair kit in my pocket, then, isn't it?" said Ava, laughing her evil laugh. She pulled it out and had fixed the hole in the bottom before the Crims could even think of an appropriate swear word.

"FIND OUT WHERE SHE BUYS HER BIG POCKET PANTS AND BUY ME A PAIR FOR MY BIRTHDAY, WOULD YOU?" Uncle Knuckles said to Aunt Bets.

"I don't buy pants from anywhere," said Ava. "They're handmade for me by tiny tailors. Who may or may not be elves—they have very pointy ears. And you'll never have your own personal elves, because you're not evil at all! You're not even unpleasant! You're actually quite heart-warming, the lot of you! You disgust me!" And with that, Ava jumped into the lifeboat and rowed speedily off in the general direction of the cruise ship, which was now completely out of sight.

Imogen felt as though she might cry, and she hated crying; it made her look weak, and she wasn't weak—she had been doing one-handed push-ups since she was five. She was marooned on an island. An island filled with deadly booby traps. Sure, she had saved her family's lives, but it was only a matter of time till one of them ate a mango filled with tiny knives and died. And then, obviously, there was the whole starving to death thing to think about. . . .

But then something unexpected happened.

Imogen heard a loud "AAAARKKK! AAAARKKK!" coming from the sky. She looked up just in time to see a huge, glowing seagull swooping down toward Ava and picking up the lifeboat in its huge beak. Then it flapped its wings and soared off into the distance.

"What was that?" asked Nick.

"Was it a mutant seabird?"

"Probably," muttered Delia. "I've always said that pouring toxic sludge into the oceans was a bad idea."

"No," said Imogen. "That's not a mutant seabird. That's a superhero. That's . . . the Gull! He's got Ava!"

The Crims looked at one another, stunned.

No one said anything.

And then Isabella smiled up at Imogen toothlessly and said, "Now what?"

"Well, I guess we're going to have to come up with

a really, really good plan," said Imogen. And then she noticed something half buried in the sand, glinting in the sunlight: Ava's phone. It must have fallen out of her pocket. She picked it up and Googled, "What should you do when your best friend/worst enemy has been kidnapped by the Gull?"

But obviously, there was no Wi-Fi signal.

Imogen looked up. The other Crims were just standing around, staring at her. "Isn't anyone going to help me?" she said.

And then Delia turned to Imogen and said, "I don't think Isabella meant what are we going to do about Ava," she said. "I think she meant, what are we going to do about *you*?"

IMOGEN LOOKED AT Delia. And then she looked at the rest of her family, who had formed a terrifying circle around her. They all looked quite angry. And by "quite angry," I mean "frothing at the mouth and looking around for rocks to murder her with."

"You were going to maroon us on this island?" said Big Nana, in a terrifyingly steady voice. "After we came to save you from Ava?"

"I didn't *need* saving," said Imogen. "Me and Ava were doing just fine before you came along and ruined everything."

"Imogen and Ava, sitting in a tree," said Delia, in a singsong voice.

"What are you, three years old?" asked Imogen. She sat down on a plank of the shipwreck. "Look," she said, "I told you. I wasn't going to maroon you forever. I was going to pick you all up as soon as me and Ava had defeated the Gull!"

"But, darling," said Josephine, "what would have happened if you *hadn't* managed to defeat the Gull?"

Imogen sighed. "I just sort of assumed we would defeat him," she said. "I mean, this is Ava we're talking about."

"Yeah," said Delia. "The girl the Gull just plucked out of the ocean and has probably already eaten."

"I hadn't really thought it through," said Imogen.

Big Nana shook her head. "I taught you better than that," she said. "And I taught you better than to abandon your family on an island to starve to death or be eaten by jaguars."

"That isn't necessarily what would have happened!" Imogen said desperately as her family closed in on her. "Don Vadrolga might have taken pity on you and let you live in his horrible pink mansion! It could have all ended happily!"

"Except it didn't, did it?" said Big Nana. "And now we're all marooned on this island. And those jaguars are probably pretty hungry. And Don Vadrolga isn't even here anymore. So he can't take pity on us."

"Except that he didn't lock his back door, so we can all just go and hang out in his house and eat his food till we figure out how to get out of here," said Freddie.

"Good point," said Big Nana.

But Imogen wasn't going to stand for this. She wasn't going to let her family make her out to be the villain when Big Nana was the one who had lied to them all and led them on this mad treasure chase. "Ava was right about one thing," said Imogen.

"The fact that navy-blue bikinis are more flattering than bright pink ones," Josephine said with a nod.

"No!" said Imogen. "The fact that you all hold me back! All the time! We wouldn't be in this mess if you had just let me go off with Ava and have one adventure on my own!"

"But Ava's a psychopath!" said Delia. "What if something had happened to you? You're our family, and families should stick together. Like we stuck with Big Nana after she faked her own death! Like we stuck with Josephine after she signed us up for that stupid TV show! Like we stuck with YOU, after you refused to believe the Kruks were after us last autumn!"

"Then you should still stick with me!" said Imogen.

"Everyone makes mistakes! Especially Crims! It's what we do best!"

"The thing is," Al said sadly, "it doesn't seem as though you *want* us to stick with you."

Imogen's face fell. Her father was right. She had wanted to get away from her family. But not *permanently* . . .

Big Nana sat down next to Imogen and put her arm around Imogen's shoulders. "Let's go and have a little chat, shall we?" she said. "Give the others some time to cool off."

"I don't need time to cool off," said Delia. "My feelings aren't going to change. You want to go it alone? FINE! Be like that! Look what happens when people leave girl bands! They have REALLY UNSUCCESSFUL SOLO CAREERS!" And she turned away and stomped across the sand toward the rain forest.

"Let's go with her," said Sam, beckoning the other Crims. "She's probably heading to Don Vadrolga's mansion. Maybe we'll find something that can help us get off this island. He's the sort of person who might have a spare sixteen-seater helicopter lying around somewhere."

Imogen and Big Nana were alone. And when Big Nana was angry, she was a very dangerous person to be alone with. But she didn't look that angry anymore.

"I understand how it feels to be frustrated by your family," she said. "Clyde, Al, and Bets are my children.

Do you know how many times I've asked myself, 'What did I do wrong?' Why does Al end up opening a savings account every time I send him to rob a bank? Why can't Clyde pickpocket a child on the way home from school without spending three years drawing up detailed plans for how to do it, involving steps like 'Teach dog how to talk' and 'Figure out how to disguise self as a paving stone'? Why does Bets only murder people with tiny sharp household objects? It's so messy to clean up with her afterward . . . but that doesn't matter. Because I love them. And I *need* them. And you're going to be the head of this family one day," said Big Nana, patting Imogen's hand, "which means that you're going to need them too. Even if you can't stand to be in the same room as them sometimes, even if you want to throw them all down the garbage disposal, and the only reason you don't is that the garbage disposal smells when it gets clogged up. You're going to have to learn how to work with them, just like you learned how to work with Ava. And let's face it, she's an *actual* psychopath."

"I know," said Imogen. "She's really proud of it. She's actually the treasurer of the International Psychopath Association. They don't have meetings IRL anymore because every time they met up, at least half of them ended up dead."

Big Nana shook her head. "And yet you trusted Ava more than you trusted your family? Really?"

"It's not that I trusted her," Imogen said slowly, and not altogether truthfully. "It's just that I wanted to commit a half-decent crime, and I thought she'd be able to help me do it."

"But you've seen what the Crims can do when we work together," said Big Nana. "We're so much stronger together than you are alone. Even though you've got a blackbelt in karate and an encyclopedic knowledge of poison antidotes."

"Ava's not all bad," said Imogen.

"Oh, I know!" said Big Nana. "She pushes you to be better! And she was right about one thing: You should never let a superhero win anything, except one of those fake 'You've won a million pounds!' contests that fraudsters use to scam people. The Gull is about to realize how wrong he was not to be afraid of the Crims."

Imogen looked at her grandmother. "You mean—we're going to try to fight the Gull and save Ava?"

"That's exactly what I mean," said Big Nana. "As long as we can persuade the rest of the family. Because right now, they aren't your biggest fans."

"I know," said Imogen. "I left my biggest fans on the cruise ship. I had two battery-powered ones in my bedroom, and they kept me really cool in the hot weather."

Imogen followed Big Nana through the rain forest, dodging the machine-gun palm trees, and the poisonous lake, and the lethal boomerang disguised as a butterfly, until they came to Don Vadrolga's mansion. Imogen felt her heart speed up as they walked across the manicured lawn to the front path. Maybe all wasn't lost. Maybe she could get her family back, and save her dangerous but strangely lovable friend, and defeat a superhero all at once.

They walked into the marble hallway and looked around for the other Crims. "Hello?" called Imogen.

Delia stepped into the hallway, her arms crossed. "Decided to join us, have you?" she said. "Look what I found when I was going through the drawers in the living room, looking for a stray Golden Globe Award." She handed Imogen a business card.

The business card smelled strongly of sardines and seemed to be printed on a whitish feather. There was writing on the front:

GULL PERSONAL SECURITY SERVICES
NOTHING SAYS KEEP OFF LIKE A GIANT SEABIRD
POOPING ON YOUR HEAD

"So," said Big Nana. "The Gull is the one protecting this island."

"Which means that Vadrolga is in with the Gull," said Imogen. "Which means that he might have helped him plan his attack on Krukingham Palace. It was an inside job!"

"Oh who cares about that—" said Delia.

But before she could say any more, Imogen heard an incredibly loud sucking noise, followed by a cackle—the sort of sound a vacuum cleaner would make if it were huge, and could fly, and was able to laugh. And then, from somewhere above them, they heard a voice shouting, "COMING IN HOT!"

THE MUSSEL WAS back.

Imogen headed for the front room of the mansion, which was decorated with photographs of Don Vadrolga's eyes, so it felt as though he were staring at them from the walls— It was quite disconcerting. Delia and Big Nana ran in after her, and they all crowded around the window, to see what the Mussel was doing.

He was outside in the front garden, hovering above the hedge shaped like the talking baby, spraying the flower beds with his squirt guns. "Where are you?" he shouted. "Are you tired of fighting me? Have you got . . . Mussel fatigue? Ha! Ha!"

"His puns have improved," said Delia, "but a superhero should never laugh at his own jokes."

"That's right, my jammy dodger," said Big Nana. "Where are the others? They're not outside, are they?"

"I think they're hiding out in the bedrooms," said Delia. "They were trying on all of Don Vadrolga's suits before you got here."

Imogen watched the Mussel, who was still spraying water all over the garden. He was pretty much just watering Don Vadrolga's plants for him. "It really is insulting that the Gull keeps sending this guy to fight us instead of attacking us himself," she said.

"Maybe the Gull will come and fight us, if we defeat the Mussel," said Big Nana. "So how are we going to do that?"

"I have an idea," said Delia. She ran out of the front room and reappeared a few minutes later holding three Super Soakers.

"Where did you get those from?" Imogen asked.

"Don Vadrolga's game room!" she said. "It's mostly just Don Vadrolga–themed stuff in there—Don Vadrolga Monopoly; a Scrabble set where only Don Vadrolga catchphrases win points . . ."

"But he doesn't have any catchphrases," said Imogen.

"That's probably why there weren't any letters in the box, then," said Delia. "But it looks like Don is a big fan of water fights! There are loads of water pistols in there. And a water cannon, and a bow and arrow, for some reason."

Big Nana called the rest of the family downstairs. They weren't pleased to see Imogen, but they were more concerned with defeating the Mussel than fighting among themselves. There would be plenty of time to hate Imogen when they got back to Blandington.

Delia handed out the water weapons. Nick and Nate each grabbed a water pistol. Imogen went for the cannon. Big Nana decided to wield the bow and arrow. And everyone else grabbed Super Soakers.

"Right," said Imogen, loading a water balloon into the cannon. "Everyone ready?"

"Crims assemble!" shouted Henry.

"That isn't our motto," said Imogen.

"May the odds be ever in the Crims' favor!" said Nick.

"Nor's that," said Imogen.

"Nothing is more important than family! Except dinosaurs!" said Big Nana.

"That's the one," said Imogen. "Unfortunately. Everyone ready? Three . . . two . . . one . . ."

"ATTACK!" shouted Uncle Knuckles, and he led the Crims outside. They ran into the garden, shooting water in all directions—but the Mussel was nowhere to be seen.

"Quiet, everybody," Imogen said. "I think I can hear his jet pack engines. . . ."

The sound seemed to be coming from somewhere above the mansion. She looked up at the roof—and that's when the Mussel sprayed a great waterfall of water at her. Imogen fell to the ground, trying to scramble to her feet, but the water kept on coming.

"You can't treat my granddaughter like that," said Big Nana, loading her bow. "Even if she *is* a traitor who wanted to leave us all for dead."

"Sorry about that," said Imogen.

"Apology accepted," said Big Nana. And she fired an arrow straight at the Mussel.

But the Mussel dodged out of the way. And the arrow fell back down to Earth and ripped through Josephine's fur coat.

"Gravity defeats us once again," murmured Uncle Clyde.

"My coat is *ruined*!" wailed Josephine.

"Serves you right for wearing fur on a tropical island," said Delia.

"Back inside the house for a huddle!" cried Big Nana.

The Crims gathered around Big Nana in the living room.

"I think it's time for an inspirational speech," said Big Nana.

Everybody groaned. They hated being inspired.

"Who are we?" asked Big Nana, pacing up and down in front of her family.

"The Crims," said Uncle Clyde, looking very pleased with himself for getting the answer right.

"And what do we do?" asked Big Nana.

"We try to commit crimes, but mostly, we just sit around and argue and burn crumpets," said Henry.

"Not the answer I was looking for," said Big Nana.

"We stick together," said Delia.

"Exactly," agreed Big Nana, pointing at Delia. "And when we stick together, what can we achieve?"

"Anything!" said Al.

"Well, maybe not *anything*. Let's be real. But we can achieve *some* things," said Big Nana. "And we certainly aren't going to let a superhero dressed as a giant booger defeat us. Are we?"

"No!" shouted the Crims.

"So, let's go out there. And let's show the Mussel who's boss."

"Who's the boss?" asked Henry. "Ava?"

"NO!" shouted Big Nana. "We, collectively, are the boss! And we're going to take the Mussel down!" She hoisted the bow and arrow onto her shoulders. "Ready?" she shouted.

"Yeah!" the Crims shouted back. And they ran out

of the mansion, in slow motion. And then they sped up, because the Mussel was already firing his water pistol at them.

The Mussel was hovering above the roof of the mansion now. Imogen aimed the pistol between his eyes, the way Big Nana had always taught her. She got a direct hit.

"Nooooo!" shouted the Mussel. "My eyes!"

"Well, mussels have about thirty-six eyes," said Delia. "So just try looking out of some of your spare ones."

"Someone's been reading the 'mussel' Wikipedia page!" said Big Nana.

"What's so impressive about that?" said the Mussel. "Wikipedia pages are notoriously unreliable. I should know—I edited that one myself!"

"I knew baby mussels didn't really attach themselves to fish, like parasites, until they're big enough to survive on their own. . . ."

"No, that bit's true," said the Mussel.

"Gross," said Delia.

"Sorry to interrupt," said Big Nana, "but we have a water fight to be getting on with." And she fired another arrow at the Mussel—and managed to hit his jet pack.

"Good shot," said Imogen.

The Mussel started flying around and around in great looping circles.

"This is our chance," whispered Imogen. "He's weak

now. Uncle Knuckles, climb up onto the roof and attack the Mussel from behind, while we keep shooting at him from below to distract him."

"OKAY!" shrieked Uncle Knuckles.

"Quietly," said Big Nana.

"NOT A PROBLEM!" screamed Uncle Knuckles. He ran around to the back of the house, the ground shaking every time one of his massive feet hit the grass, and started climbing up the rear of the mansion.

The Mussel stopped flying around in circles for a moment. "What are you lot planning?" he asked. "Your funerals, I hope!" And luckily, he laughed so hard at his terrible joke that he didn't notice Uncle Knuckles clambering up the side of the mansion with all the subtlety of a major earthquake.

"Come down here and fight us, if you think you're hard enough!" said Uncle Clyde.

"Nice try, weird human!" said the Mussel, flying higher, toward the chimney.

Behind him, Uncle Knuckles was clinging to the chimney like a bad remake of *King Kong*. He gave the other Crims a thumbs-up and did that bunny ears thing behind the Mussel's head, just for fun.

"How dare you call me a human!" shouted Uncle Clyde.

"Nice," Big Nana whispered to Uncle Clyde. "Taking

offense at everything—great distraction technique."

The Mussel was clearly trying and failing to come up with a great comeback—Imogen recognized his facial expression, because it was the one she pulled when she was trying to work out the vocative of a tricky Latin verb—and while the Mussel was thinking, Uncle Knuckles let go of the chimney and leaped onto him.

Imogen stared, openmouthed, as the two men fell through the sky and landed on the grass with a sickening crack.

"UH-OH," said Uncle Knuckles, standing up. "WAS THAT MY NECK?"

"No!" wailed the Mussel, writhing around on his back. "It was my shell! My beautiful shell!"

"Get over it," said Delia, standing over him. "It's not *that* beautiful. What's it made of? Papier-mâché?"

"Yes, as a matter of fact," said the Mussel. "And now I'm all squishy and vulnerable!"

"That's right," said Big Nana. "And now it's time for us to have a lovely French meal."

"Ooh," said Uncle Clyde. "What are we having? Beef Bourguignon?"

"No, you idiot. Mussels *marinière*."

"Please don't eat me!" said the Mussel. And then he stopped speaking, because a shower of roof tiles crashed down on top of him like very heavy raindrops.

Imogen checked that the Mussel was still alive—he was—and then she stood back and looked down at him, feeling the lovely sense of accomplishment that she always felt when someone she didn't like was weeping and calling out for their mother.

Nick and Nate hauled the Mussel to his feet and dragged him across the garden to Don Vadrolga's hot tub. They handcuffed him, turned the Jacuzzi to "Dangerously Hot," and added some white wine and garlic for good measure.

"The bubbles! I can't take the bubbles!" cried the Mussel, who looked quite old up close—about seventy, maybe, with a peace sign tattooed on his wrist and too many earrings for someone over retirement age.

"Nice ink," said Henry. "Where did you get it done?"

"I'll tell you, if you turn the heat down," the Mussel said desperately.

"Okay," said Henry reaching for the controls. But Big Nana slapped his hand away.

"Nice try, Mr. Mussel."

"It's not Mr. Mussel. Just the Mussel. Otherwise, I sound like a household cleaner, and that's not really what I was going for—"

"Whatever," said Big Nana. "We'll only turn the Jacuzzi bubbles down once you've told us where the Gull's island is."

"Never!" wailed the Mussel.

"Okay," said Big Nana, turning the bubbles up to "Lethally Frothy."

"Yeah!" said Sam. "Let's crack the Mussel!"

"I'm melting!" cried the Mussel.

"Actually, you're just cooking," said Big Nana.

"But I'm not ready to die! I've never seen the Grand Canyon!" he wailed. "I've never ridden a camel! I've never been on a yoga retreat!"

"I HAVE!" said Uncle Knuckles. "IT WAS WONDERFUL. THE VEGAN FOOD WAS DELICIOUS."

The Mussel started to cry.

"Great," said Sam. "His tears will add salt to the water. The perfect seasoning."

"Okay, okay!" said the Mussel. "I'll tell you where the Gull's island is."

Big Nana's hand hovered over the Jacuzzi controls. "We're listening," she said.

"It's not far from here," said the Mussel. "Just take a left at the shipwreck, sail north for an hour, and you'll see it."

"How are we going to sail there, though?" asked Freddie. "We don't have a boat."

"Don Vadrolga has, like, three Jet Skis and a speedboat in his private harbor," said the Mussel.

"Okay," said Imogen, handing him Ava's phone. "Program the directions into the GPS, and we'll let you go."

Hands shaking, the Mussel entered the coordinates into the phone.

Imogen nodded to Big Nana, who turned off the Jacuzzi, and the twins dragged the Mussel out onto the grass.

"I'm so ashamed," said the Mussel, weeping. "I'm a terrible sidekick. I'm not cut out for this! I have the soul of an artist!" He pulled off his Mussel costume. Underneath, he was wearing tie-dyed swimming trunks. He ran through the garden—hotly pursued by the Crims, because they didn't know where Don Vadrolga's private harbor was, and they were hoping he was heading there—and jumped into one of the Jet Skis.

"Where are you headed?" jeered Sam. "Going to retire to Barbados and sell your paintings on the beach?"

"How did you know?!" said the Mussel.

He started up the Jet Ski and disappeared into the distance.

The Crims cheered and high-fived one another. But Imogen caught Big Nana's eye, feeling worried. How was she going to convince them to save Ava from the Gull?

"I'm so glad he's gone!" said Josephine, flopping down onto the grass. "Now that that idiot's out of the way, I say we take over the house and stay here for the rest of the summer. I'm longing to try out his spray tan booth. You can never be too spray tanned, you know."

"Actually," said Imogen, "There's just one little thing we need to do first. . . ."

"Yes! Find something to eat!" said Uncle Clyde.

"No, actually," said Big Nana, putting her arm around Imogen's shoulders. "We need to save Ava from the Gull."

It's fair to say that the Crims didn't take the news well. There was some weeping. A fair amount of shouting. A couple of attempted murders.

"There is NO WAY we are putting our lives on the line to save that SELFISH BRAT," said Delia. "Ava deserves everything she gets. Except that Best Supervillain Under 30 Award she got from the International Association of Supercriminals last year."

"Look," said Imogen. "I know she's selfish. And stuck up. And irritating. And sadistic. And weirdly fond of Justin Bieber. But she's a criminal. And we have to side with criminals over heroes. Otherwise, what does that make us?"

"Law-abiding citizens," Uncle Clyde said thoughtfully.

"Exactly," said Imogen.

The Crims all grunted. Which she took to mean "You're right, Imogen. You can count on us."

"Come on," she said. "Let's go back up to the house and make a plan."

"As long as we can eat something before we go," said

Uncle Clyde. "Don Vadrolga has pepperoni pizzas in his freezer."

"Sure," said Imogen. "There's probably even time for a quick spray tan."

The Crims all crowded into Don Vadrolga's kitchen and feasted on frozen pizzas and microwave macaroni and cheese. Everyone was in a much better mood once they'd eaten. As Isabella was gnawing on everyone's leftover crusts, and also their ankles, Imogen told them her plan. It didn't take long, because she didn't have a clue how they were going to rescue Ava.

"First we need to find out more about the Gull's lair."

Delia laughed. "What, are you planning to call up the Gull and ask him to send you the blueprints?"

"Close," said Imogen.

She pulled out Ava's phone and logged into Don Vadrolga's Wi-Fi (the password was pretty easy to guess: Don-Vadrolga-is-a-very-underrated-actor). And then she loaded Skype and dialed the International Association of Supercriminals. Before too long, a balaclava-clad head appeared on the screen.

"Yes?" said the head.

"Hello!" said Imogen, in her head-girl voice, which probably wasn't the most appropriate voice to use when calling a criminal organization, but she was a little flustered. "It's Imogen Crim here, and I was wondering what information you can give me about the Gull's lair. My family is about to rescue Ava Kruk—"

"What's your membership number?"

"I don't actually have a membership number—but I come from a very old crime family. The Crims. Our membership pack probably got lost in the post. The postman doesn't really like coming to our house, because of the snakes."

"Sorry," said the head, "but if we let *you* into the International Association of Supercriminals, we'd have to let every single twelve-year-old pickpocket in. We have to have *some* standards." And the connection went dead.

Imogen fumed. "How *dare* they dismiss us like that?" she said.

Delia held out her hand. "Let me have a go," she said. Imogen handed the phone to Delia.

"What are you doing?" asked Imogen.

But Delia held up a hand to silence her. "Making a voice call," she mouthed. "Hello?" she said out loud, in her whining Ava Kruk voice. "Is that the IAS? Yeah—Ava Kruk here. That total *amateur* Imogen Crim just grabbed my phone off me, so I drowned her in a puddle."

Imogen gave Delia a thumbs-up. *I really should give Delia more credit,* she thought. *She's devious, reckless, and brilliant at lying—all the qualities you could ask for in a cousin.*

"Yeah, great," Delia was saying in her whiny voice. "Could you send across the blueprints to the Gull's lair? Great. And any other useful information you have on him—his favorite color, what he eats for breakfast, how he kills his enemies, that sort of thing. You've sent it across already? Thanks! You're so efficient!"

Imogen gave Delia a very quiet high five.

"One more question," said Delia. "Imagine if the Crims did manage to destroy the Gull—I know, ridiculous idea, right? But go with me for a second. Imagine, somehow, that they pulled it off. What kind of reward would they get for that?"

Imogen heard a hanging-up noise on the other end of the phone. *Typical Delia,* she thought.

"They hung up on me!" said Delia, pouting.

"But you've got the blueprints, right?" asked Imogen.

Delia checked Ava's email. "Yes!" she said. "But I should warn you—this lair looks pretty well-defended."

"That's okay," said Imogen. "We'll think of something. . . ."

"Will we?" said Delia.

"Yes," said Big Nana. "It just might not be the *right* thing."

IMOGEN, DELIA, AND Big Nana sat around Don Vadrolga's kitchen table, which was shaped like the underground bunker from Vadrolga's worst-reviewed sci-fi movie, and came up with a plan. It was quite a simple plan—it involved stealing Don Vadrolga's speedboat, driving to the Gull's lair, and saving Ava somehow. Sure, that last bit was a bit vague, but they figured they'd improvise. They had started taking improv lessons at Mildly Amusing, Blandington's most mediocre comedy school, so they were good at thinking on their feet. It wasn't hard to persuade the rest of their family to go along with it. As Sam had said, "If I have to play one more Don Vadrolga–themed game or watch one more Don Vadrolga movie, I'm going to die. Either that, or I'll move to Hollywood, grow my hair into a ponytail, and start going to the gym a lot, which would be worse." Plus, none of them had ever been on a speedboat before.

They all piled into the boat, and Isabella sat on Uncle Clyde's lap and steered as Delia read out the directions from Ava's phone. Imogen looked around at her family—Josephine's hair was whipping in the wind; Freddie's shirt-sleeves were whipping in the wind; Aunt Bets's whip was whipping in the wind (she was striking the side of the speedboat as though it were a horse, shouting at it to go faster). Imogen felt another rush of love for them all. She did enjoy doing things with them, really. She just didn't like going on vacation with them to horrible campsites.

"I'm bored," said Henry, flicking his lighter.

"How can you be bored?" asked Imogen. "You are literally on a speedboat, racing toward a superhero's lair. It's like you're inside a computer game."

"Yeah, but I've played that one before," said Henry.

"Great," said Delia. "So, you can tell us how to defeat the Gull when we get there."

"Are we nearly there yet?" asked Sam, stroking his pet hedgehog.

Imogen looked out at the horizon. "Actually, I think we are," she said. There was an archipelago in the distance—a series of rocky white islands, arranged in a semicircle. They reminded her of something, but she couldn't work out what, exactly.

Seeing the islands cheered the Crims up a bit. Henry put away his lighter. Sam put away his pet hedgehog. Aunt Bets put away the kitchen knife that she had been threatening to stab Sam with if he poked her with his hedgehog one more time. Everyone sat up straight. Focused, serious. Imogen started to feel a little more confident. *We can do this,* she told herself.

Delia told Isabella to park the speedboat next to one of the two central islands. These two were taller than the other islands, and strangely square. And carved out of the rock was a huge, shining castle. With no obvious entrance.

"We can't get any closer than this," Delia said to Imogen in a low voice. "If we do, the boat will run aground, and we'll have no way of escaping."

"Okay," said Imogen. "We're going to have to swim to shore. Has everyone got their life jackets on?"

The other Crims nodded. They had found them underneath the seats of the boat—a dozen life jackets with Don Vadrolga's grinning face printed on their fronts and backs.

Imogen zipped the blueprints they'd printed out to the Gull's lair in a waterproof folder—Big Nana had always told her, "You never know when you'll need a waterproof folder. In an emergency, you can even poke holes in it and use it as underpants"—and tucked it inside her swimming costume.

Pretty soon, all the Crims had sploshed into the water and doggy paddled to shore. Nick and Nate took a bit longer than everyone else, because they wanted to practice doing forward rolls in the water, but soon, they were standing on the rocks, looking up at the huge, white castle.

Imogen pulled the blueprints out of the waterproof folder. "There's a door into the basement somewhere close to the waterline . . . ," she said.

"It's here!" said Sam, running over to a tiny doorway. He pushed the door. "It's locked. Who's got a skeleton key with them?"

"Me!" said every single other Crim. Except Al, who tried to avoid skeletons of all kinds.

Sam took Josephine's key and jimmied the lock. The door creaked a little as he pushed it open, and, one by one, the Crims walked into the castle.

Imogen squeezed through the door last, and shut it behind her. It took a while for her eyes to adjust to the darkness of the basement after the glare of the sun outside. But even then, there wasn't much to see—the basement was pretty boring, as most basements are, unless they're incredibly terrifying.

She took the blueprints out of the plastic folder and studied them. "There's a room on here marked 'DUNGEON/

AUDITORIUM.' I'm guessing that's where the Gull is holding Ava prisoner. So let's head there first. And once we've rescued Ava, we'll need to destroy the castle."

"DO WE ACTUALLY NEED TO DESTROY THE CASTLE, THOUGH?" asked Uncle Knuckles. "BECAUSE THAT SOUNDS QUITE DANGEROUS, AND I'D PENCILED IN A MEDITATION SESSION AT TWO O'CLOCK, SO I'D LIKE TO GET BACK FOR THAT."

"Yes, we do," said Imogen, "because the only way the International Association of Supercriminals will take us seriously is if we bring the Gull down."

"FINE," said Uncle Knuckles. He sighed (and accidentally set off a tornado in Kansas).

Delia looked over Imogen's shoulder at the plans to the castle. "It looks as though the basement is the lair's weak point," she said.

Imogen nodded. "This is where the electricity generator is, and the telephone cable—plus, it says here that the castle has very weak foundations. So, if we fire directly at the basement with Ava's cannon, the whole castle will be destroyed."

"But we don't *have* Ava's cannon," said Sam.

"Actually," said Imogen, pulling the small but deadly weapon out of her pocket, "we do."

The Crims gave her a round of applause.

Imogen hushed them. "Shhh," she said. "You can praise me silently. Bow, curtsy, whatever."

Once the bowing was over, Imogen led her family out of the basement and into the castle itself. It was beautiful, in a strangely white sort of way. The walls were white, and the carpets were white—the Crims tiptoed across them, trying and failing not to leave dirty footprints behind—and for some reason, the walls were decorated with colorful pop art pictures of soft foods. Imogen saw an oil painting of scrambled eggs outside the bathroom on the first floor, and a huge mural of an avocado on the second-floor corridor, and a massive poster of a tub of plain yogurt on the third-floor landing.

"Is it me," she said as they crept up another staircase, "or does this whole place smell like toothpaste?"

"I think it's more like mouthwash," said Uncle Clyde, walking headfirst into a wall. Probably because he was scribbling in his notebook instead of looking where he was going.

"This isn't the time to develop your watercolor skills," said Imogen.

"I'm not!" he said. "I'm trying to keep track of where we are in relation to the blueprints." He looked down at his drawing and pointed to a pale pink door that led off the corridor. "Here," he said. "This room should be the auditorium."

Imogen pushed the door open. But it wasn't the auditorium—it was a living room, completely upholstered in pale pink: the soft carpet on the floor, the pillowy sofas, and floor cushions—even the walls and the ceiling were covered in a squashy-looking pink fabric.

"It looks like a marshmallow," said Nick.

"Or that pink Ralph Lauren gown Gwyneth Paltrow wore to the Oscars that time," said Josephine. "I should know. It's hanging in my closet at home."

"Or . . . the inside of a mouth?" said Al.

Uncle Clyde looked at his drawing and gasped. "You're right!" he said. "It *does* look like the inside of a mouth! And the whole castle—in fact, the whole island—is shaped like a tooth!"

Imogen looked down at the blueprint again. Uncle Clyde was right. "So *that's* why I keep thinking about oral hygiene," she muttered. She turned to the blueprint that showed the whole archipelago, and gasped. Together, the islands made up an entire set of teeth. "This makes perfect sense," she said. "*That's* why the basement is the most sensitive part of the castle—because the nerves in your mouth are underneath your teeth. And this room looks like the gums—"

"Because it's directly above the basement," said Uncle Clyde, nodding.

"Right," said Imogen. "What we need to do is perform a root canal on the castle. We need to drill directly down into the basement from this room and aim for the weak foundations. That way, we have a good chance of bringing the whole castle crumbling down."

Al raised his hand. "I have a question," he said, adjusting his glasses. "Your plan is an excellent one—your plans always are! Have I mentioned how proud I am to have you as my daughter?"

"Yes. But I always like hearing it," said Imogen.

"But if we really do manage to hit the weak foundations and destroy the whole castle, how are we going to get out alive?"

"We'll just need to brace ourselves," said Delia. "Get it?"

"We all know the drill," said Sam.

"Please don't brush off my concerns," said Al.

"Well, I find this whole plan unnerving," said Josephine.

"Okay," said Imogen. "Enough of the terrible puns. First things first. Let's not worry about destroying the castle right now. First we've got to rescue Ava. So let's try to find the dungeon/auditorium. Everybody ready?"

"Yes!" chorused the Crims.

So, Imogen pushed the pink, padded door open—and came face-to-face with two security guards.

The security guards were wearing white coats—like dentists, Imogen realized. One of them held a walkie-talkie up to his mouth and said, "We've found the cavities. Repeat: We have found the cavities."

Imogen pointed the cannon at the other security guard, but he managed to snatch it. Then he turned it around and pointed it at her.

"What are you doing here?" asked the security guard.

"Let me fill you in," said Sam, whose pun skills actually improved when he was under pressure.

"No need," said the other security guard. "We know who you are. We have orders to take you to see the Gull."

Imogen swallowed. It was like Big Nana had always told her: "If you find yourself staring down the barrel of a cannon, you'll know that you have made some very bad decisions, and you probably won't have time to put them right."

Dear The IAS,

Just wanted to check on that reward again for when we defeat the Gull. P.S. thx for the WWASVD bracelet.

—Delia

16

EVIDENCE

A FEW VERY unpleasant minutes later, the Crims were lined up in the huge, empty dungeon/auditorium. It was more auditorium than dungeon, really—there were banks of seats up each side of the room, like a high school gym, and although there were a few cages at the far end, they were empty. There was also a water slide leading from the auditorium out into the ocean below, which Imogen thought was a good sign. People who enjoyed water slides were usually quite lighthearted and not very good at hurting people. Imogen wondered what the Gull used the room for when he wasn't sliding out into the sea. Seabird-themed superhero conferences? Lycra-based fashion shows? And then she wondered: If this was the dungeon, then where was Ava?

But then she stopped wondering, because a huge video screen flashed into life at the other end of the hall. The Gull appeared on the screen, flapping his ridiculous (but very effective) homemade wings. "Thmo," he said. "Thme meet mat mlatht."

"What did he just say?" Delia whispered to Imogen.

"I think he was trying to say 'So we meet at last,'" she said. "Must be hard to talk with that stupid beak attached to his face."

"Is it a real beak?" Nick whispered.

"Or has he had plastic surgery?" asked Nate.

"I'd love to have plastic surgery," Josephine said wistfully. "Just a couple of tweaks and tucks, and I think I'd look just like Princess Grace of Monaco. When she was alive. But why you'd want to make yourself look like a mutant duck, I have no idea."

"To stay on brand," said a voice from above them.

Imogen looked up—and there, dangling from the ceiling in a tiny cage, was Ava.

"Are you okay?" Imogen mouthed. But Ava looked away. She obviously hadn't forgiven Imogen for choosing her family over her. *You think she'd get over it, seeing as I've risked my life to come here and save her,* Imogen thought. But the Kruks considered "grateful" to be such a dirty word that they employed a censor to beep it out of their favorite TV shows, along with words like "helpful," "friendly," "kind," "honest," and "Malala Yousafzai."

"Smo. Smi smave moo min smy sums," said the Gull.

The Crims looked at him blankly.

"Mmm smpose smoo—"

"Oi. Bird Face," said Ava. "No one has any idea what you're trying to say."

The Gull groaned with frustration. He reached behind him, picked up an iPad, and started to type, turning the tablet around so they could see what he had written.

So. I have you in my grass at last.

The Crims looked at one another. "We're not in your grass," said Nick. "We're in your auditorium."

The Gull groaned again. *That was a typo,* he wrote. *Meant to write "grasp," not "grass."*

"Ohhhh," said the Crims, nodding.

"Must be quite hard to type when you have wings instead of fingers," Aunt Bets said sympathetically.

The Gull nodded and started typing again. *I've been witching you—*

"Witching?" said Uncle Clyde. "Is that another typo?"

"Or maybe he's really a witch!" said Josephine. "That would explain how he ended up with that horrible beak! Probably a spell gone wrong!"

The Gull shook his head. *Sorry! Autocorrect!* He took his

arm out of the wing part of his costume and tried again. *I've been watching you for months.*

"Ohhhh," said the Crims again.

"So, we're *not* beneath your notice, then," said Josephine. "But in that case, why have you been sending your pathetic sidekick to deal with us, instead of attacking us yourself? It's so disrespectful! We've appeared on national television, you know!"

The Gull laughed at that—at least, he tried to laugh, but the beak made it quite difficult, so it came out as a sort of smug, suffocated wheezing sound. *I* have *been attacking you,* he typed into his iPad. *Indirectly. You're the ones I'm really after. Not Ava. Everything I've done since I became a superhero has been designed to lure you to my island.*

Imogen couldn't help smiling up at Ava triumphantly. This wasn't good news, obviously—really, the fact that a deranged, bird-faced superhero had targeted her family was very, very bad news indeed and would probably result in at least one death or a lot of prison sentences—but this meant that as far as the Gull was concerned, the Crims were more dangerous than Ava. And Delia was obviously thinking the same thing, because she stuck her tongue out at Ava and whispered, "See? People do know who we are. He was just using you to get to us! Who's the loser now?"

Ava pretended not to hear. She was sitting in her cage,

her arms crossed, a disgusted look on her face. Though that might have been because Uncle Knuckles was nervous, and when Uncle Knuckles was nervous, he sweated. And when Uncle Knuckles sweated, he smelled like a clogged garbage disposal.

I don't know what you're so happy about, typed the Gull. *But you won't be smiling after you've seen this. . . .*

The Gull disappeared from the screen. His face was replaced by shaky camera footage of the Gull and the Mussel, standing in what looked like a tiny warehouse, surrounded by confused-looking people in black polo shirts. The Gull kept giving orders that no one could understand, and the Mussel kept translating them for him.

"Make sure they don't suspect a thing," said the Mussel. "They have to think that they're actually *good* at stealing laptops."

The confused-looking people burst out laughing.

"Good one," said the one with frizzy hair.

I recognize her . . . , thought Imogen. And then she noticed the label on her shirt: "Mega Deals."

Imogen felt sick. "So, you set up the Mega Deals heist?" she asked the Gull.

The Gull reappeared on the screen. He nodded as triumphantly as someone can when their entire face is hidden by a beak.

"But that doesn't make any sense," said Delia. "The

Mega Deals heist was set up by the TV producers from that stupid show—"

But then the Gull disappeared again, and more shaky-camera footage flashed up on the screen. This time it showed the Gull sitting in a meeting room with Belinda Smell, the overexcited TV producer from EZTV.

"This is a win-win situation," Belinda was saying to the Gull. "You get to lure these criminals to your lair. We get must-watch television. It'll do wonders for our ratings! Gum?"

The Gull shook his head sadly and pointed to his beak.

Imogen sighed. This was all too much. She just wanted to go home alone and eat an entire tub of chocolate ice cream. But unfortunately, she was very far from home, and she was the opposite of alone, and every time she looked at the door marked "EXIT," one of the security guards pointed a gun at her and said, "One move, and we end you."

"Hang on," said Freddie, scratching his head. "The Gull can't be behind the TV show. The whole thing was Josephine's idea. Which makes much more sense, because I've done the numbers, and she's responsible for two out of every fifteen stupid decisions this family makes."

Everyone looked at Josephine. The Gull appeared on the screen again. *Why don't you tell them how you came up with the idea for the show*, he typed into his iPad.

"Well," Josephine said slowly, "now that I think about

it, the idea to apply for the TV show came to me in a dream . . . a very vivid dream. I dreamed a huge bird with a speech impediment came into my bedroom and handed over the EZTV registration forms. . . . And now that I come to think of it, I wasn't actually asleep at the time."

Big Nana cuffed Josephine around the head.

Josephine stared at Big Nana, shocked. "Al, darling!" she said. "Are you just going to let your mother treat me like that?"

"Yes," said Al. "Sorry, dear, but you deserved that."

And that's not all! typed the Gull. He disappeared again, and a montage flashed onto the screen. There were the Crims stealing the donation cup from the *Punch and Judy* show—and there was the Mussel, behind the scenes, operating the *Punch and Judy* puppets. There were Nick and Nate, buying ice creams on the rainy pier—and there was the Gull, his beak hidden behind a mask, taking their money. And there was Delia, leading the donkey home from the beach. Except it wasn't a donkey at all—it was the Gull in a pantomime donkey costume.

"*You're* Mavis?" Delia was horrified. "How could you treat me like this when I fed you so much delicious hay?"

The Gull reappeared on the screen. *I ate hay!* he typed.

"I know you did," said Delia. "That's what I just said."

I mean, I HATE hay, typed the Gull. HATE HATE HATE HATE HATE—

"MAKE HIM STOP!" cried Uncle Knuckles. "I GET VERY ANXIOUS WHEN PEOPLE TYPE IN CAPITAL LETTERS!"

The Gull laughed his strange, wheezing laugh. *You, Knuckles Crim, are pathetic. And so are you, Josephine Crim. And you, Al Crim. And you, Delia Crim. And you—*

"Right, we get the idea. We'll be here all day if you type every single name out," said Freddie.

"If you think we're so pathetic, why did you go to so much effort to lure us to your island?" asked Imogen. "Wait—did you blow up Krukingham Palace just to get our attention?"

Ava groaned from above.

I did indeed. Don Vadrolga made it easy! See, I don't think you're all *pathetic*, wrote the Gull. *Just most of you. One of you is an evil genius. One of you is my true nemesis.*

Imogen couldn't be positive—the beak made it hard to tell who the Gull was looking at—but she was pretty sure he must be talking about her. She felt a flush of pride. *I'm a superhero's nemesis!* And then a flash of fear. She had been enjoying not having a nemesis. . . .

But then she realized that the Gull was actually looking at . . . Freddie.

Freddie looked as surprised as she felt. "Me?" he asked. "What have I done? I spend most of my time doing the cryptic crossword these days!"

These days, that may be true. But what about in the old days? Before you knew Big Nana was still alive?

"I ran an illegal poker ring. But only about ten people ever played, and everyone was sworn to secrecy— Did Blabbermouth Bill tell you about it? I should have known not to trust a man with a name like that. I've never met a Bill who didn't try to deceive me."

Guards! Bring him forward! typed the Gull.

The security guards marched up to Freddie, grabbed him by the shoulders, and pushed him toward the screen. Imogen hadn't noticed before, but the guards were wearing surgical gloves . . . She shivered. What was the Gull going to do to Freddie?

Freddie stumbled to a stop in front of the screen. The Gull smiled down at him. At least, he attempted to smile. It's hard to smile when you have a beak.

So, typed the Gull. *We meet again.*

"We really haven't met before," said Freddie. "I never forget a face. Particularly not a giant one, covered in feathers."

Do you recognize me now? asked the Gull—and he pulled off his mask, beak and all.

Josephine sighed with relief. "At least we don't live in a world where someone would sew a beak onto their face."

"Shh!" said Delia, pointing at the screen. "Look who it is!"

Imogen stared, openmouthed, at the Gull's real face. He was scrawny, with messy brown hair and strangely sunken lips. "It's you!" she whispered.

"That'th right," said the man on the screen. "It'th me . . . UNFORTUNATE PETE!"

The other Crims gasped.

"Er, excuse me," said Ava from above their heads. "Can someone please explain to me who Unfortunate Pete is?"

"He—he used to be in my secret poker ring," said Freddie, his voice shaking. "And he wasn't very good at poker, so he ended up owing me loads of money. And because he couldn't pay me back, I made him punch himself in the face. And unfortunately, he knocked all his teeth out. But how could I know that was going to happen?! I didn't know he had such an effective uppercut! Or such loose teeth!"

Big Nana tutted. "I always knew that poker ring was a bad idea," she said. "But I was too dead to do anything about it."

"Hang on," said Freddie, turning around to look at Big Nana. "How did *you* know about my secret poker ring?"

"WHO CARETH?" screamed Unfortunate Pete, who was slightly easier to understand without the beak. "Focuth on ME for oneth, Freddie! You ruined my life! And now it'th time for me to get my revenge. I've reinvented mythelf ath the Gull, becauth seagullth are the motht terrifying creatureth on Earth, even though they have no teeth!"

"I have to disagree with you there," said Freddie. "It's statistically proven that the deep-sea anglerfish is the most terrifying creature on Earth. It's just that it lives so deep in the ocean that people aren't terrified by it that often."

"No one wanth to hear your thupid thahtithicth!" said Unfortunate Pete.

"What did he just say?" Delia whispered to Imogen.

"THUPID THAHTITHICTH!" said Unfortunate Pete, spraying the camera with spit.

"It's statistically proven that 'statistics' is the most difficult word to say if you don't have any teeth," said Freddie.

"THUT UP!" cried Unfortunate Pete. And then he smiled. "Actually, don't. Becauthe it'th time for me to *make* you thut up. . . ."

Josephine ran toward the screen and fell to her knees. "Please!" she wept. "Spare us! We have done no wrong! Take Freddie, if you must—he never does his share of vacuuming—but let the rest of us live!"

"Oh, I don't care about the reth of you," Unfortunate Pete said dismissively. "You're free to go. The cruithe thip ith waiting downthairth. There'th a round of piña coladath waiting for you in the bar area."

"THAT'S VERY THOUGHTFUL OF YOU," shouted

Uncle Knuckles as Uncle Clyde ran past him to the exit, "BUT HAVE YOU PROVIDED NONALCOHOLIC OPTIONS FOR THOSE OF US WHO ARE TEETOTALERS OR UNDER THE LEGAL DRINKING AGE?"

Imogen watched her family push and shove one another out of the way in their hurry to get out of the auditorium/dungeon.

"Save me a lounger!" Nick called to Nate, who was closest to the door.

"The Jacuzzi is mine!" shouted Big Nana.

But Imogen didn't move. "Wait!" she called.

Everyone waited.

"We can't just abandon Freddie," she said.

"We definitely can," said Delia, who already had her hand on the door. "That's *exactly* what we're about to do."

"But how would you feel if you were in his position?" Imogen asked her.

"Uncomfortable, probably," said Delia, looking at the way the security guards had folded Freddie's arm behind his back.

Imogen turned to the Gull. "What are you planning to do to him?"

"You're about to find out," said the Gull, and he laughed an evil laugh. Except he wasn't actually evil, so really it was just a laugh. "Guardth!" shouted the Gull. "Put Freddie into . . . THE THUIT!"

"The chute?" asked one of the security guards, pointing at a water slide.

"NO! THUIT!"

"You want us to shoot him?" asked the other security guard, cocking his pistol.

"NO!" shrieked Unfortunate Pete. "Dreth him in the thuit with the teeth!"

"The suit with the teas?"

"TEETH!" shouted Unfortunate Pete, trying to bare his teeth to show them what he was talking about, but he didn't have any teeth, so it didn't really work.

Freddie rolled his eyes. "I think he wants you to dress me in that suit over there," said Freddie, pointing to a pink jumpsuit that was laid out in a corner of the stage. It was covered with mechanical fake teeth.

"Why didn't he just say so?" asked the guard, patting Freddie on the back. "Thanks! You're a real gent!"

"Any time," said Freddie.

The security guards picked up the suit and handed it to Freddie. "Do you just want to go ahead and put this on yourself? It's probably easiest that way."

"Sure," said Freddie. He zipped the jumpsuit up and stared down at the plastic teeth.

He looked ridiculous, but looking ridiculous wasn't much of a punishment for Freddie—he owned more than one Hawaiian shirt.

"Are those teeth suppose to . . . do something?" Imogen asked the Gull.

The Gull shook his head. "Don't tell me the thuit's out of batterieth. . . ."

"Don't worry!" said the security guard. "I picked some up at the supermarket this morning! They were on special." He loaded them into the battery pack that was sewn into the waistline of the jumpsuit and flicked the switch to "CHEW."

Immediately, the plastic teeth started opening and closing, trying to chew Freddie.

Freddie wriggled and started laughing. "It tickles!" he said.

"That looks mildly annoying," Big Nana whispered to Imogen. "But really nothing that Freddie doesn't deserve."

Ava laughed so hard that her cage rattled. "You call THAT a punishment?!" she asked.

"Yeth," said the Gull, looking a bit put out.

"Ha!" said Ava. "You're not a superhero. You're not even a hero. You're just a weirdo who can't even eat solid foods."

"Yeah!" said Henry.

"QUIET!" shouted the Gull. He turned to the Crims. "Why are you all thtill here?"

"We're not leaving till you let Freddie go," said Imogen. "And Ava, too."

"You can take Ava. I've had enough of her," said the Gull. "Guardth! Releathe the prithoner!" he cried.

The guards opened Ava's cage—and she jumped down to the floor and ran straight out of the dungeon/auditorium without looking back. "So long, suckers!" she called over her shoulder.

"Freddie too," insisted Imogen.

"Freddie ithn't going anywhere," said the Gull. "And becauthe you all thought hith punithment wath tho pathetic, I'll try a different one." He smiled and turned to Freddie. "Which of your relativeth would you like to be killed firth?"

"I've actually thought a lot about this," said Freddie without hesitation.

"All right, never mind," said Big Nana. "We're leaving. What is it I always tell you, children? 'Never overstay your welcome. Unless you're at an all-inclusive resort.'" And she ushered the other Crims out of the auditorium.

Imogen was the last to leave. She looked at Freddie, still laughing and writhing around in the stupid jumpsuit, like an extremely toothy worm. She didn't want to leave him alone. But if this was the worst punishment the Gull could come up with, then he was going to be fine . . . wasn't he?

The Crims were unusually quiet as they walked back to the cruise ship.

"What if Unfortunate Pete actually kills Freddie?"

Imogen whispered to Big Nana.

"He won't," Big Nana said. "Unfortunate Pete isn't a supervillain. He'll just irritate Freddie a bit and then let him go. We should just let the poor guy have his fun—after all, he can't even eat a sandwich without putting it into a blender."

"Okay," said Imogen. "And we'll swing by tomorrow to pick Freddie up?"

"Exactly, my single-use toothpick," said Big Nana.

"And we should track down Ava, too," said Imogen. "Who knows what she'll be plotting next. . . ."

Imogen boarded the cruise ship and collected her piña colada from the bar area. She walked to the upper deck and lay back on her favorite lounger. It was strange, being back here without Ava. But also quite relaxing, she had to admit. Delia walked past her, a copy of *Goodbye!* magazine in her hand. Imogen patted the empty lounger next to her.

"Come and sit with me," she said.

But Delia just huffed and walked to a lounger on the other side of the pool.

Imogen sighed. There was a reason "holding a grudge" was listed in the special skills section of her cousin's résumé.

Imogen settled back, closed her eyes, and listened to the relaxing birdcalls. But then her eyes snapped open again. Because she had just heard a very unrelaxing bird-call indeed.

A horrible *ARRRK . . . ARRRK* was coming from the sky above her. Imogen looked up and saw the Gull, clutching Freddie in his prosthetic talons, flapping his impressive wings, flying her cousin to a strange-looking structure on top of the castle.

"Is that . . . a catapult?" Delia asked.

Imogen nodded. "I just assumed that was how he launched himself into the sky to fly. . . ."

The Gull strapped Freddie into the catapult. Then he programmed a digital timer on the side. Imogen recognized it—she'd stolen the exact same model during the Mega Deals heist.

The timer flashed: "30 MINUTES." And then the countdown began. . . .

"Is it me," said Delia, pointing off to the right, "or is that catapult aimed at that tall, spiky island?"

"It's not you," said Imogen.

"That tooth is the canine in the dental archipelago," said Aunt Bets, who was swimming laps in the pool; she knew a lot about teeth.

"THWEDDIE LMIVED BMY THME THMOOTH, THMO HME'LL DMIE BMY THME TMOOTH!" screamed the Gull, who was wearing his ridiculous beak again.

"None of us have any idea what you're talking about," yelled Delia.

"I think he's trying to say that I lived by the tooth, so I'll die by the tooth," called Freddie.

"Thmank myou," said the Gull.

"You're welcome," said Freddie.

The digital timer flashed "29 MINUTES."

"I have a horrible feeling that this punishment is going to be slightly worse than the strange, toothy jumpsuit," said Imogen. "We have to help him."

"But how?" said Delia. "We either need a jet pack or some wings. Or, like, a time machine, but I don't think we're going to find one of those in the sports equipment store, even though it is unusually well stocked."

"I don't know," said Imogen. "But we have to figure it out, fast. Or Freddie is going to be impaled on an island."

IMOGEN CALLED THE other Crims to the pool deck. "We need a plan," she said.

"I need earplugs," said Sam as the Gull circled above the ship, AAARRRKing in victory.

"Well, I need a new piña colada," moaned Josephine. "The ice in this one has melted. Honestly, the service on this boat has absolutely *nothing* on the Pitz." (The Pitz was a luxury hotel in Blandington, which Josephine enjoyed being thrown out of.)

Uncle Clyde raised his hand.

"Yes?" said Imogen.

"I have a plan!" he said. "First we need to find out

how to turn water into gold. Then—"

Imogen held up her hand to stop him from speaking. "Sorry," she said. "I should have been clearer. We need a plan that will actually *work*."

"Oh," said Uncle Clyde, disappointed.

The timer on the catapult flashed "25 MINUTES."

"Duh," said Delia, hands on her hips. "It's obvious what we need to do. We have to shoot the Gull out of the sky. So, what are we waiting for? There are loads of weapons on this ship!"

"NMOT ANY MNORE!" shrieked the Gull. "I CONFITHCATED THEM ALL! HA! HA! HA!"

Freddie waved at them from the top of the catapult. "Sorry to butt in," he yelled across at them, "but would you mind hurrying up? There are only twenty-four minutes left on the timer. Plus, the Gull's screeching is really hurting my ears."

"I've got it!" Big Nana said suddenly, jumping out of the Jacuzzi like a very spritely old woman, which is what she was.

"What have you got?" Imogen said hopefully. "The cannon? An anti-aircraft gun?"

"No," said Big Nana. "This." She ran to the kitchen and came back with one of the pineapples from the *Golden Bounty*. It was rotten now, and flies were buzzing around it like planets circling a revolting sun. "We just need to find a way to fire these at the Gull, and we can shoot him out of the sky."

"I have an idea," said Al, running to his cabin. He came back with the telescope he used to study the stars. (Apart from accountancy, astronomy was Al's biggest passion in life. He liked lots of other things beginning with *A*, too, including apples, the aristocracy, and Alabama.) He pointed the telescope at the Gull's catapult and studied how it was put together. "I think we could build our own catapult out of things we have on this ship," he said. He snapped his telescope shut and started giving orders, the way he had during the pirate attack. "Henry," he said, "you're good at finding matches, even when I've confiscated them. I want you to find every single flammable thing on board this ship."

"Aye-aye, Captain," said Henry.

"Nick and Nate," said Al, "go and get the chairs from the dining room. Knuckles, you bring me the karaoke machine. But DON'T USE IT! Sam, help Isabella bite all the elastic out of the fitted sheets. And Delia, bring me the individual chocolates from everyone's pillows. I could use a snack."

The Crims rushed around, bringing the things Al had asked for to the pool deck. Most of the Crims that is; Uncle Clyde and Josephine had drunk so many piña coladas that they were now snoozing on their loungers, as if a grisly murder involving a giant tooth wasn't about to take place before their very eyes.

"Honestly," said Big Nana, shaking her head. "I would disown them, if I didn't like owning things so much."

Imogen, Delia, and Big Nana went to the bar area and picked up armfuls of rotting pineapples. By the time they had piled them all up on the deck, Al and the others had managed to build something that actually looked like a catapult. "It's a Crimacle!" said Big Nana, standing back to admire it. (A Crimacle is the Crims' equivalent of a miracle—it's when something that the Crims try to do actually works. A very unusual occurrence.)

"Right," said Al, loading a pineapple into the catapult. "Time to test it." He swiveled the catapult around until it was facing Josephine, who was snoring loudly from the lounger on the other side of the pool.

"You wouldn't," said Imogen.

"I would," said Al.

Imogen was impressed—her father seemed to have gotten a lot braver in the last few months. A lot more authoritative. Perhaps he had learned a thing or two from the Kruks while they were holding him hostage. Perhaps he and the rest of the family had more to offer Imogen than she'd given them credit for. . . .

Al paused to polish his glasses. Then he pulled back the catapult, and the pineapple flew through the air toward

Josephine, like a spiky, decomposing bird.

BOING! The pineapple bounced off Josephine's forehead. *SPLAT!* The pineapple rebounded and hit Uncle Clyde smack in the face.

"Hooray!" cheered the Crims. Apart from Josephine and Uncle Clyde, who had jerked awake and were now staring around them, terrified.

"The Gull!" cried Josephine, rubbing her head.

"He got us!" said Uncle Clyde, picking pineapple spikes out of his hair. "Wait . . . why are you lot all laughing?"

"GUYS!" Freddie shouted across at them from the catapult. "I can see you're having lots of fun down there, and I'm happy for you and everything, but you have less than twenty minutes to save my life. The odds of you managing to save me are now under twelve percent. . . ."

"Good point," said Al. And he swiveled the catapult around and aimed it at the Gull. "Nick and Nate," he muttered, "get ready to climb Freddie's catapult and untie him, when I give you the all clear. And Imogen—pass me a pineapple. . . ."

"NINETEEN MINUTETH, THIRTHY-THIX THECONDTH!" shrieked the Gull.

"Wait!" begged Freddie. "Please don't kill me! There's so much I haven't done! I'm so close to finding a cure for death and developing the perfect blueberry muffin recipe. . . . If you let me go, I'll write a one-man show about how terrifying and impressive you are, and dedicate it to you—"

"I hate one-man thowth!" cried the Gull.

"I don't blame him," Delia whispered to Imogen as Al fired the catapult. "Do you remember Freddie's last one-man show? About his toenails?"

"No," said Imogen. "I've had a lot of therapy to block it out. . . ."

Al fired the catapult—and missed. "Ha!" laughed the Gull. "Ymou cman't cmath me! Amd ymou monly hathme eightmeen minuteth to thmave Frmeddie'th mlife!"

"Again!" yelled Big Nana—and this time, when Al fired a pineapple, it knocked the Gull off-balance.

"Keep them coming!" said Al. He fired another pine-apple at the Gull—and missed.

"Quick!" shouted Imogen. "Another one!"

There was one pineapple left. Al took a deep breath, and fired—and this time the pineapple hit the Gull's right wing, punching a hole in the feathers.

"YMOU'LTH MNETHER TAKE ME MALITHE!" screeched the Gull, flapping his wings—but only the left wing worked, and it wasn't strong enough on its own to keep him in the air, and he was spiraling down through the sky, toward the ocean. . . .

"Dead's fine, too," said Delia as the Gull plunged headfirst into the water.

"Quick! Get me down from here!" called Freddie. The timer was still counting down . . . Just seventeen minutes until he was fired at the canine-shaped island.

"Nick and Nate are on the way!" called Imogen.

Nick had jumped onto Nate's shoulders, and he was already climbing up the outside of the catapult. He reached out a hand and pulled Nate up behind him. (They were the best climbers in the family; they had kidnapped a mountaineer when they were eight and forced him to teach them to abseil, boulder, and sing all the words to *The Sound of Music*.) But when they reached the top of the catapult and tried to free Freddie from the harness, they couldn't get him out.

"Just disable the timer!" said Freddie.

Nick grabbed the timer on the side of the catapult and smashed it on a rock, but it kept counting down, as if it was wearing a party hat getting ready to celebrate New Year. "There's a keypad on the timer," said Nick. "There must be a code to turn it off. . . ."

Freddie started to cry. "It's no good," he said. "In less than fifteen minutes, I'm going to be stuck on that tooth like a nasty bit of spinach you can't get rid of. It serves me right for being so intelligent and good at poker." He looked down at his family. "Can you forgive me for being so talented?"

"We're not giving up yet," said Imogen. "We still have a few minutes till the timer goes off. We'll just have to get the Gull to tell us the code to disable the timer and the catapult."

"But the Gull is dead!" wailed Freddie.

Al looked up from his telescope, which was trained at the patch of ocean where the Gull had fallen. "He's not," he said. He passed the telescope to Imogen. She looked through it, and sure enough, the Gull had pulled himself onto the rocky shore, and he was lying there, twitching and flapping his good wing.

"I have an idea!" said Imogen.

"Ooh," said Uncle Clyde. "Have you figured out a way to make bread toast itself?"

"No."

"Is it a way for us to become really good at golf, so we get lots of money in sponsorship, without actually having to practice, because it's really boring?"

"Please stop guessing," said Imogen. She put down the telescope and looked around at her family. "We need to turn the Gull's own fears against him," she said. "What does he think is the most terrifying creature on the planet?"

Big Nana clapped her on the back. "Imogen. You are brilliant! Like a very stolen diamond! Come on everyone. We're going to get the Gull!"

"Quickly as you can," said Freddie. "Twelve minutes left . . ."

💣 💣 💣

Imogen ran into the sports equipment store and came out carrying a scuba suit. "Here," she said, tossing it to Henry. "Put this on and go and get yourself some snacks from the poolside bar."

"But, Imogen, darling," said Josephine. "You know Henry always gets food all over himself when he eats. . . ."

"That won't be a problem," said Imogen. "Now. Who wants to come and get the Gull?"

"Me!" said Aunt Bets, brandishing her hatpin.

"Okay," said Imogen. "But remember we need him alive."

"Then I'm not interested," said Aunt Bets.

"I'll come with you," said Delia.

"Me too," said Sam. "I have a few more seabird puns I'd like to try out on him."

By the time Imogen, Sam, and Delia reached the Gull, he had passed out and was lying sprawled across the pebbles like a failed paper airplane, with a huge pineapple-shaped bruise on his face.

Imogen looked back at the timer on Freddie's catapult. Less than ten minutes left . . .

"Quick," said Imogen. "Let's get this stupid costume off him!"

Sam and Delia pulled the Gull costume off Unfortunate

Pete. He was wearing nothing underneath but a pair of Kitty Penguin boxer shorts.

"Look! You have the same taste in music!" Imogen said, nudging Delia.

"Eww," said Delia, screwing up her face. "She is so last year."

Imogen looked around for Henry. "Where *is* he?" she said. "There are less than nine minutes left on the timer!"

"Here!" shouted Henry, running up the beach. As Imogen had hoped, the scuba suit was now covered in fries and ice cream and candy, a hot dog bun, hamburger relish . . .

"Perfect," said Imogen. "Now take that off and dress the Gull in it."

Henry looked horrified. "Take it off?" he said. "But I've just got underwear underneath!"

"It can't be as embarrassing as his," said Delia, pointing to the Kitty Penguin boxer shorts.

But Henry's underwear turned out to be just as embarrassing as the Gull's. Because when he peeled off the scuba suit, he too was wearing Kitty Penguin boxer shorts underneath. "Kitty Penguin is my guilty pleasure," he mumbled. "Just like Delia's is helping old people cross the road."

"Hey," hissed Delia. "You promised you'd never tell anyone that!"

"I really want to make fun of you both right now," said Imogen, "but I don't have time." She grabbed Unfortunate Pete under the armpits. "You guys take his legs," she said. "Let's carry him to that rocky area near the shallow water. . . ."

They dragged Unfortunate Pete over to a rock pool and dropped him in the water. Then backed away to see what would happen.

Which, unfortunately, was nothing.

"Five minutes till I die!" cried Freddie. "Four minutes fifty-nine seconds . . . fifty-eight . . . What have I done to deserve this?!"

"Lots of things," said Imogen. But she crossed her fingers and muttered, "Please let this work . . ."

"Great plan, Imogen," Delia said. "What were you expecting to happen?"

A second later, a seagull started to circle overhead. And then another. And then another . . .

ARRRRRKKKK! ARRRRRKKK! they cried . . .

"Yesssss," hissed Imogen, as one by one, the seagulls flew down and landed on Unfortunate Pete's scuba suit, and started to peck. . . .

Imogen shook Unfortunate Pete awake. As soon as he saw the birds, he screamed. "Get them oth me!" he shrieked.

"No problem," said Imogen, standing over Unfortunate Pete with her arms crossed, as the gulls fought over a hot dog bun. "If you tell us how to turn off the timer, we'll help you out."

She looked at the timer. She had less than two minutes to save her cousin's life. This had to work. . . .

"Do you think I'm that gull-ible?" said Unfortunate Pete.

"You can give the puns a rest now," said Sam.

"If I die, you'll be gull-pable!"

"Seriously, we don't actually like Freddie that much," said Delia. "We can always just walk away . . . and leave you to be eaten . . . by the most terrifying creatures on Earth. . . ."

"Okay!" cried Unfortunate Pete. "Thith ith the code to turn the timer oth: DON'T GAMBLE WITH THE GULL."

Nick climbed back up to the top of the catapult and started typing the code into the timer. "You couldn't have come up with something shorter?" he asked.

"TEN SECONDS" flashed the timer.

It took Nick five seconds to work out where the key to type in the apostrophe was . . .

But he found it just in time.

And just as the timer flashed "ONE SECOND," it went dead, and the harness on the catapult clicked open. Freddie stood up and gave Nick a hug. "You saved me!" he said.

"Actually, we all did!" Imogen shouted up at them from the shore.

"Yeah!" called Uncle Clyde from his lounger on the pool deck.

"Except you," Imogen called across to him.

Imogen and Delia tied Unfortunate Pete up and marched him back onto the cruise ship. "Well," she said as she opened the door to the cabaret theater and pushed him inside. "That was certainly all resolved very neatly."

But she had spoken too soon. Because the next minute, a huge flame symbol flashed into the sky. And the minute after that, a fireball came hurtling toward the cruise ship out of nowhere. As it landed on the deck, and picked itself up, and dusted itself off, and adjusted its perfect ponytail, Imogen realized it wasn't a fireball after all. It was . . .

"Ava!" Imogen cried.

But there was something different about Ava. Actually, there was a *lot* different about her. Her ponytail, though still perfect, was also on fire, and she had actual flames licking up and down the sides of her red jumpsuit, which Imogen could only assume was made of some sort of flame-retardant fabric. Ava threw back her head—Uncle Knuckles, who was standing behind her, had to jump out of the way to avoid getting burned—and laughed the evilest laugh

Imogen had ever heard. And with every "Ha!" smoke and flames spurted out of her mouth, as if she were a very intelligent, very unpleasant dragon.

"As you can see," said Ava, "I have reinvented myself. I am the ultimate solo supervillain. My name isn't Ava anymore. I answer to . . . the Flame."

Imogen could see the terror she felt reflected in her family's eyes. All except Henry's. Because he was staring at Ava with undisguised adoration.

"Now I understand what Kitty Penguin meant when she sang 'I love you more than I love playing computer games in my pajamas,'" he breathed. "I think I'm in love!"

BEFORE HENRY COULD declare his love to the Flame, and before the Flame could fireball everyone to death, a speedboat pulled up next to the cruise ship, splashing everyone and temporarily putting out the flames on Ava's legs. On board was a TV crew, filming them. Imogen read the logo on the side of the cameras: "EZTV."

"Wait," said Imogen, turning to Josephine. "The reality show crew is back? *Why?*"

But Josephine was reapplying her lipstick and pretending not to hear.

Belinda Smell waved at the Crims from the speedboat.

"Hello!" she called. "Just carry on with what you were doing. Pretend we're not here."

"Couldn't you just go away?" said Imogen. "That way we wouldn't have to pretend."

"Sorry," said Belinda. "Could you say that again? I've trained myself to hear only positive, uplifting things."

The rest of the EZTV crew started unloading their kit from the speedboat—cameras, monitors, director's chairs, clapper boards, and doughnuts.

"Er, excuse me?" said Ava. "Who *are* these badly dressed people? And why aren't they paying me more attention?"

Belinda Smell handed Ava a business card. "Belinda Smell. Executive producer, EZTV," she said. Ava breathed on the card, and it burst into flames.

"I'm so confused," Imogen said. "Why are you still interested in us? The whole reality TV show was orchestrated by the Gull! And he got what he wanted—he lured us to his lair. So what are you doing here? And how did you know where to find us?"

"I left them a voicemail, telling them that we were living it up in the Caribbean and having some very juicy, TV-worthy moments!" said Josephine. "Which we still would be, if we hadn't used up most of the pineapples fighting the Gull."

Belinda Smell nodded. "And our most recent show, *Pigs Might Fly*, didn't go as well as we'd hoped. Because pigs really don't like flying at all. So, we needed something to fill the airtime."

Imogen looked at Ava. The flames on her costume were bigger than ever—they seemed to feed on her anger. Imogen couldn't help being impressed. She couldn't help being terrified, either, but she was pretending not to be by casually standing with her hand on one hip and whistling the jingle from a famous ice cream commercial.

Ava turned around. "Who's whistling?" she said. "And why do I suddenly want a Klondike bar?"

"That was me. Sorry," said Imogen.

"You will be," said Ava. "Because things are about to get . . . smokin'."

Ava turned a triple pirouette—Imogen felt a stab of envy, as she'd only ever managed a double in ballet class—and used her flamethrower to force the Crims and Unfortunate Pete into a group in the middle of the deck. She pulled what looked worryingly like a length of candlewick out of the pack on her back and tied it around the Crims. And then she tucked a few sprigs of lavender into the candlewick, which was even more worrying.

"Are you turning us into a . . . candle?" asked Imogen.

Ava nodded. "I left all my travel candles at home," she

said. "And it's really hard to relax after a long day without the soothing fragrance you get when you burn your former enemies alive."

"I love you!" shouted Henry. "Set fire to me first!"

"You'll have to wait your turn, weirdo," said Ava. "Because first, it's time for . . . an evil monologue."

Ava pulled out an oversized match and struck it on the sole of her foot to light it. She started pacing on the deck in front of the Crims and Unfortunate Pete. "Your problem," she said, pointing at Pete, "is that you're terrible at staying on brand."

"Acthually, right now, my problem ith that you're about to burn me alive—" said Unfortunate Pete.

"Shut it, Bird Boy!" shouted Ava. "You were dressed up as a seagull, but all your punishments seemed to involve teeth, and then you had that ridiculous clam sidekick—"

"He wath meant to be a muthel, actually."

"But that's exactly my point! He's forgettable! There's no brand recognition!" She pointed her flaming torch at him. "Give me one word that the citizens of the world should think of when they think of you," she said.

"In charge," said Unfortunate Pete.

"That's two words," said Ava.

"Okay," said Pete. "Thafe. Becauthe I'll alwayth be there to rethcue them when they're in danger."

"Ha! 'Safe!'" Ava laughed. "That's a good one! You should go into stand-up comedy!"

"Do you think?" asked Unfortunate Pete. "Becau-the that'th another word I'd like people to connect with me—'entertaining.' And 'environmentally friendly,' bec-authe combatting polluthon ith very important to me. And 'oral hygiene,' becauthe if I'd bruthed my teeth more often, they might not have fallen out when Freddie made me punth mythelf—"

"See?" said Ava. "You're just proving my point! You don't know what you stand for! No wonder you have such a terrible catchphrase. Whereas the Flame is the ideal super-villain. I work alone, so no one can let me down or use up all the toilet paper and not replace it." She shot Imogen a look. "And I have a clear brand. It's all about fire. Speaking of which," she said, and she used her flamethrower to start shooting fireballs at the Crims. "YOU get a fireball and YOU get a fireball and YOU get a fireball," she cried like a psychopathic daytime talk-show host.

"Uh-oh," said Freddie, pointing to the end of the can-dlewick.

It was on fire.

I guess this is it, thought Imogen. *I never thought this is how I would die: tied up next to my relatives and a toothless guy who's really bad at poker, and turned into a lavender-scented candle.*

"Imogen," Big Nana whispered, "don't give up. You know what I always say: 'It isn't over until the psychopath sets fire to your hair. . . .'"

That's right! thought Imogen, remembering her criminal lessons. It was always a good idea to get your enemy to expand on his or her dastardly plans—it gave you time to come up with an escape plan. *So I just have to keep Ava talking. . . .*

"I have a question," Imogen said. "Why are you doing this? Why fire? Why the Flame?"

Ava looked at her. "What do you mean?"

"You know," said Imogen. "All really good supervillains and superheroes have got a moving origin story. Like the Joker used to be a comedian before he fell into a vat of toxic chemicals and turned into a mass murderer. And the Penguin was bullied because he was short and round and had a beak-like nose, but he reclaimed his nickname and dressed in black and white when he turned to crime and fought Batman. So, what's your deal, Ava? What fire-based trauma do you have in your past?"

Ava pouted. "Well," she said, "everyone hates fire, right?"

"I don't," said Henry.

"But you don't have a really *personal* reason for choosing fire as your brand," said Imogen. "Which means you aren't a real supervillain. Because *real* supervillains have heart. They're motivated by pain and anger and a desire for warped justice. You just decided to be the Flame because you thought fire would be an easy brand to sell!"

"That's not true!" said Ava, but the flames on her costume had started to dwindle.

Imogen noticed a pineapple lying on the deck near Sam's legs. Sam had managed to wriggle his arms free from the candlewick and was reaching out to grab it. Ava hadn't noticed yet. Imogen just needed to distract her for a little bit longer. . . .

"Okay, then," said Imogen. "Give me an example of a terrible fire-related incident from your past. And I'm not talking about the time that Elsa forgot to buy candles for your birthday cake."

"But that was really upsetting!" said Ava. "No one sang 'Happy Birthday' to me at all that year! I'm going to—"

But we'll never know what Ava was going to do. Because before she could finish her sentence, Sam hurled the pineapple at her.

The pineapple hit Ava's head.

And she fell backward and smacked her head again on the deck.

"Ava?" Henry said anxiously. But Ava didn't reply, because it's hard to reply when you're unconscious.

"The Flame is out!" cried Sam. "Repeat: The Flame is out!"

"Hooray!" cried the Crims.

"Noooo!" cried Henry.

Sam managed to free the others from the candlewick and stamp out the flame.

Josephine looked around, disappointed. "The camera crew have disappeared!" she said. "They didn't get *any* of that!"

"Maybe they were burned up into cinders by a fireball," said Imogen.

"Some people get all the luck," said Henry.

Imogen tied Ava up using her candlewick, and Isabella sailed the cruise ship back to the Gull's lair, so they could lock her in the dungeon/auditorium. Freddie and Imogen carried her out of the cruise ship and up to the castle—but as they were hauling her up the white staircase, Ava awoke.

"Nice going, losers," she said, trying to wriggle free. "You managed to knock me out. With a piece of fruit. I didn't expect that. Credit where credit's due."

Imogen ignored her. "Let's put her in that strange cage that dangles from the ceiling again," she said, as they maneuvered Ava into the dungeon/auditorium. "She can't escape from that one. And to think I actually wanted to *save* you."

"Ha!" laughed Ava. "I'll escape from any cage you decide to lock me in! Just like Uncle Dedrick and Violet managed to escape police custody! They're going to come and rescue me. They'll be able to find me, because of the GPS on my phone."

"What?" said Imogen, pulling Ava's phone out of her pocket. "This one, you mean?"

"Nice one," said Freddie, nodding approvingly.

"Give that back!" screamed Ava.

"No," said Imogen, slipping it back into her pocket. She looked at her former best friend and current nemesis and sighed. This wasn't how she thought things would end with Ava. She had hoped that they'd travel the world together, fighting superheroes, committing crimes without even trying, drinking nonstop fruit smoothies, and listening to nonstop Justin Bieber (okay, that bit wasn't quite so appealing, but she'd been hoping to convert Ava to Rachmaninoff's piano concertos eventually). If only Ava hadn't been so fond of trying to kill her family. If only Imogen hadn't been quite so fond of her family, and so anxious to stop Ava from killing them. It could have been the beginning of a beautiful friendship. . . .

Imogen smiled at Ava. "Let's go, Freddie," she said, and turned toward the exit.

"Wait," Ava called.

Imogen turned around. Ava was standing at the bars of her cage, looking smaller and less powerful than usual.

"You have so much potential, Imogen," Ava said. "But

as long as you stick with your family, you'll never become a true supervillain."

Imogen hesitated. She wanted to be a supervillain very badly. And she couldn't help liking Ava, despite everything.

"Come on," said Freddie. "Everyone's waiting for us."

Imogen looked at Freddie, and she remembered everything they had been through together—all the failed heists and the ridiculous plans and the kidnappings and the near-death experiences involving butlers and sharks—and she thought about her other cousins and her mad aunt and uncles, and her strange but lovable parents, and her insane genius of a grandmother, and she realized that even though they definitely, definitely did hold her back, she could never leave them. "I'm fine with just being a notorious criminal," she said to Ava. "That way I get to be myself, instead of giving myself a stupid nickname. Plus, I look terrible in Lycra." She turned to go.

"Wait!" Ava called again. "Can't you turn the TV on before you go, so I have something to watch?"

"No problem," said Imogen. She walked over to the giant screen and turned it on—and then she flicked through the channels until she found what she was looking for.

Ava watched in horror as the host announced the start of a Don Vadrolga movie marathon. "No!" she screamed as the opening credits of the talking baby movie started to play.

Imogen paused in the doorway, watching. "I guess we'll never know what happened to Don Vadrolga," she said.

"He won't be able to evade the Kruks forever," muttered Ava, putting her hands over her ears.

Imogen smirked and turned up the volume on the TV. And then she and Freddie walked out of the dungeon/auditorium, ignoring the cries of "Please! Talking babies make me break out in a rash!" and "Heartwarming plots give me migraines!" and "No, please! He's wearing sunglasses! Make it stop!"

AS IMOGEN AND Freddie were walking back to the cruise ship, they passed Unfortunate Pete, sitting alone on the beach, looking more unfortunate than ever before. Freddie ran back onto the ship as fast as he could, but Imogen hung back to talk to Pete. She felt sorry for him. After all, because of Freddie, he'd lost all his money, his teeth, and his self-respect. And now he'd lost his amazingly successful second career as a superhero.

"Hey," she said. "If you don't have any immediate plans, do you fancy coming back to England with us? We have a lot of spare rooms in our house. And a bouncy castle, which is great for venting your anger, before you do something stupid like reinventing yourself as a bird and trying to murder someone with a jumpsuit covered in plastic dentures."

Unfortunate Pete smiled at her. At least, he tried to smile, but he didn't have any teeth. "Would you mind dropping me oth in Barbadoth, on the way?" he said. "I really mith Dave."

"Dave?"

"Aka the Muthel," said Unfortunate Pete.

"Oh! I always wondered what the Mussel's real name was," said Imogen. "And nice use of 'aka,' by the way. I've always wanted to say that out loud."

The Crims all agreed to give Unfortunate Pete a lift. He seemed a lot more chilled out after his pineapple-induced concussion. That night, after Sam's ten p.m. karaoke show, he joined Imogen and Big Nana in the Jacuzzi.

"I wanted to tell you how thorry I am for everything I did," he said. "I thould never have lithened to Don Vadrolga. I thould have known he couldn't be truthted."

"That's okay," said Big Nana. "It's like I always say: 'It's hard not to trust a celebrity with a chin dimple.'"

Pete nodded. "I realithe now that I wath never cut out to be a thuperhero," he said. "I want to live a thimple life from now on: live in a hut on the beath; open a thmoothie thtall, maybe—"

"Good idea," said Imogen. "Everyone, good or evil, loves a smoothie."

"Ethactly," said Pete. "And Barbadoth ith the world'th number one dethtination for budget dental work! Dave told me he'th met a great dentitht, out there, called Dr. Payne. He'll do your dental work for free if you let him perform ethperimental medical techniqueth on you. What could pothibly go wrong?"

Imogen was a little bit sad to see Unfortunate Pete go when they arrived at Barbados. And a little bit relieved, too, because he'd discovered the onboard casino and had challenged Freddie to a game of blackjack. When they left, Unfortunate Pete waved to them from the dock.

"Don't ever come back to Blandington, or I'll kill you!" Freddie said cheerfully. "I may kill you, anyway," he muttered, as the ship pulled away, rubbing his arm, which was still covered in bite marks.

Coming back to Crim House felt strange after so many weeks away. As Imogen walked up the front path, past the piranha pond, toward the stripy front door, she looked up at the house. Despite the huge bouncy castle on top, it looked smaller than she remembered.

Big Nana put her arm around Imogen's shoulders. "Happy to be home?" she asked.

"Yes," said Imogen.

"Me too," said Big Nana. "But I'll miss the Jacuzzi. And the buffet. And the ballroom. Every home should have a ballroom, I think, unless you live in a lighthouse. It's wrong to have too much fun in a lighthouse."

"DON'T WORRY," said Uncle Knuckles, running up the path behind them. "I'VE GOT AN IDEA."

Later that afternoon, Imogen and Big Nana were drinking tea in their kitchen when they heard the *BEEP-BEEP-BEEP* of a crane coming from the back garden. They ran into the garden—and there was Uncle Knuckles, lowering the cruise ship onto the house, right next to the bouncy castle. There was a distressed clucking noise coming from the upper deck. . . .

"Oh dear," Imogen said. "We forgot about the captain."

"He'll be fine," said Big Nana. "He can live in the garden with the other chickens, and the snakes, and President Jimmy Carter. It's just a shame we can't hypnotize him to lay eggs. One would be big enough to make an omelet to feed the whole family."

"Darlings," said Josephine, bustling into the garden after them. "Have you seen this week's *Blandington Times*?" She thrust the paper at Imogen and pointed to the front page.

Imogen sat down on the back step to read the article.

STELLA STICKYFINGERS: THE PINT-SIZED THIEF STEALING PINTS OF MILK!

Blandington has seemed even blander than usual in recent months—the town's much-loved Crim family has been away on a summer vacation, and crime has dropped to almost zero. Sure, it's nice to be able to leave the house and know it will still be there when you get back. Yes, it's great to go out to a restaurant and not have a pair of identical twins steal your steak before you can eat it. But life's a little bit more exciting when you could be kidnapped at any moment and held ransom for an almond croissant! But in the past week, all that has changed: a brand-new felon has filled the Crims' extremely large, extremely stolen shoes. Her name: Stella Stickyfingers. Her age: eighteen months old. Her parents: "Extremely neglectful," according to PC Phillips, who added, "But apparently they spend all their time with their Shetland pony, Molly. And who can blame them?"

Stella Stickyfingers is the star of a new reality TV series, BAD BABY OF BLANDINGTON!!!!!!! Which is shown after nine p.m. as that many exclamation marks can traumatize younger viewers. Stella's crimes so far include theft (stealing milk from doorsteps); impersonating a police siren (she has a very piercing wail); and cat tail pulling (residents are advised to keep their pets indoors between one p.m.—when infant day care lets out—and three p.m.—when bathtime takes place. Those are Stella's peak offending hours). Sales of Stella Stickyfingers merchandise have skyrocketed in recent weeks, whereas sales of the Crims action figures have nose-dived, all except for the deep-voiced Sam Crim action figure, which customers say, "Sings a lovely version of 'Someone Like You.'"

"It's a disaster!" said Josephine, sitting down next to Imogen. "We're not famous anymore!"

"Wrong as usual, my underwhelming ham sandwich," said Big Nana, patting Josephine's shoulder. "This is *excellent* news. If the police are busy with Stella Stickyfingers, they won't be watching us anymore. And if they're not watching us, we might be able to pull off some actual crimes! After we've had a mega nap, of course. And soaked in the Jacuzzi, maybe. But first, shall we have another cup of tea?"

Al was waiting for them in the kitchen, with tea and crumpets. He had taken off his pirate costume at last and was wearing his gray suit and his white shirt and his I LOVE DECIMAL POINTS! tie.

Josephine pouted up at him. "I liked you in your eye patch," she said. "I thought you were a pirate now."

"Ooooh aarrrrrr," said Al, taking a sip of tea and steaming up his glasses. "Don't be sad, me little pirate queen. I'll always be your scurvy sea dog!"

"Ooh!" squealed Josephine, grabbing him by the hand. "Talk pirate to me!"

Imogen wanted to do something—anything—to take her mind off what was happening in her apartment. So, she went upstairs to Delia's room and knocked on the door.

"Is there anything worse than hearing your parents flirting in bad pirate voices?" asked Imogen when Delia opened the door.

"I doubt it," said Delia, sitting down on the bed. "Come in and hang out with me for a bit. We can watch *Dirty Rotten Scoundrels* and paint our nails black."

Imogen sat down on the bed next to Delia and started flicking through Nickedflix to find the movie. But then she came across a familiar-looking TV show in the Recommended for You section. . . . "Hey," she said. "Our show! There are new episodes available!"

The new episodes couldn't have been more different from the first one. This time there was no laugh track and no comedy sound effects to make them seem more stupid than they really were. This time there was scary music and dramatic camera angles and footage of the Crims running in slow motion. The TV crew had obviously survived Ava's attack on the cruise ship, and they had caught every moment of what happened next. There were close-ups of Isabella's pointy teeth. There was footage of Imogen shot from below, which made her look taller and more dangerous than she actually was. There was the dramatic moment when Imogen distracted Ava . . . and Sam knocked her out with the pineapple . . . and Imogen and Freddie tied her up and carried her off to the Gull's lair. . . .

Best of all, there was no footage of Imogen saying snarky things to her family. Because she hadn't said anything snarky at all.

"I can't believe it," said Delia as the credits rolled. "It actually makes us look as though we know what we're doing. People are going to take us seriously as criminals after this."

Imogen's phone buzzed with a message. "They're already taking us seriously," she said when she saw who the message was from. She grinned at Delia. "It's the International Association of Supercriminals," she said. "They want to speak to us about joining!" She smiled, satisfied. She had made it. She had become a supervillain, just by being herself. She didn't need a stupid brand. To celebrate, Imogen and Delia settled back into the pillows, rewound to the episode where Ava got hit by the pineapple, and played it over and over again. *Everything is exactly as it should be,* thought Imogen. She was home, where she belonged. Ava had probably escaped from the dungeon/auditorium and was almost certainly hanging out in a supervillain lair, where she belonged. Imogen was friends with Delia again. And she was surrounded by her hopeless, unstable, criminal, unreliable, completely wonderful family.

There was nowhere else she'd rather be. Except maybe in a Jacuzzi, drinking a piña colada. So, she went upstairs to the cruise ship to make one.

Acknowledgments

Thanks to my writing friends Zanna and Sarah, my wife, Victoria, and my former colleagues at Quarto Books for keeping me sane when I was writing jokes every morning before work. Thank you to the brilliant editors at Working Partners and HarperCollins, particularly Stephanie Lane Elliott, Conrad Mason, Samantha Noonan, Will Severs, Elizabeth Lynch, and Erica Sussman. Thank you to Mai Ly Degnan for drawing the Crims and making them look just as funny and terrifying and mad as they are in my head.